BILLY'S DRIFT

Books by the same author

Into the Spiral
Jet Smoke and Dragon Fire
The Shining Bridge

BILLY'S DRIFT

CHARLES ASHTON

WALKER BOOKS
AND SUBSIDIARIES
LONDON • BOSTON • SYDNEY

First published 1994 by Walker Books Ltd
87 Vauxhall Walk, London SE11 5HJ

Text © 1994 Charles Ashton
Cover illustration © 1994 Wendy Hoile

This book has been typeset in Sabon.

Printed and bound in Great Britain by
Biddles Ltd, Guildford and King's Lynn

British Library Cataloguing in Publication Data
A catalogue record for this book is available from
the British Library.

ISBN 0-7445-2486-5

J137, 791
£10.15

"The dog at the furthest point of his arc–
As many strides outward, so many back."

For Linda – ten years later

CONTENTS

Package 1

Hobart

Roger,

Here's Chapter 1. See what you think of
it first.

Theresa

CHAPTER
1

SMOKE

Geordie Gibbon whirled his jacket and brought it down with a whack onto the grass. "I'm hot," he said.

"You've too much clothes on," Billy Stuart said.

"I didn't know we were coming up here," Geordie puffed. "You're all right, you never even meant to go to school today."

Billy shrugged. He had on his denim jacket and jeans and a T-shirt. You were only warm when you were in the sun unless you kept running, or climbing.

Geordie whirled his jacket and whacked it again. They were near the top of Culane Hill. The Cairn was in front of them, and the Davieburn Vale was hidden. "What would you give for a dog?" he said. "I'd give anything for a dog."

"What do you mean, what would I give?"

Billy screwed up his eyes and nose at Geordie. He was always asking stupid questions.

"I mean – what would you give to have one? I'm not getting one. Dad would let me but Mum won't." He caught his jacket on his foot and tossed it up in the air. It came down neatly draped like a cowl over his head. "I'd give any-thing. I'd give my watch."

Billy looked reflectively at the dull silver thing on Geordie's wrist. No one else had a watch like that. It could even play a tune. Geordie was always asking questions like, What if? What would you do? What would you say? He seemed to spend his life playing around with big ifs. Billy had never thought about Geordie giving his watch away before. "I'd swap you a dog for your watch," he said at length; "but I don't have a dog either."

He looked round. The sun disappeared behind the Cairn, the cold touching them immediately. Behind, the hills stretched away, ridge behind grass-covered ridge, some in shadow, some pale grey-brown, some showing crescents and slim shoulders of gold where the sun caught them. Broom bushes were dotted in the dips between the ridges, but the land was open and wild and lonely. It was the kind of place you'd go with a dog.

"No," Billy said. "I'd not swap him, not if I had a real good dog. I'd not swap him for any-thing." He was getting chilly. He turned away from Geordie, with his stupid questions. He took a run at the Cairn, reached the top in twenty strides. He was in the sun again. Davieburn Vale opened beneath him. He sat down, shading his face against the level sun. The land lay spread out in crystal-sharp detail. It was a cold, still, very bright day. There would be another frost tonight.

Geordie climbed heavily up the slope and stood looking down into the sandy slot that led from the top of the Cairn into the under-ground chamber. "Like the crack in your bum," he said, as he always said when he saw it. Then he murmured, "I wonder what it was like getting buried at the top of a hill in those days."

Billy clicked with annoyance. "Same as get-ting buried now. You're dead, so you're not caring where you're getting buried. You should have stayed at school if you want to ask questions."

"I was just wondering," Geordie said cheer-fully.

"You're always just wondering," Billy answered sourly. "Boy Wonder." He felt under him, realized the seat of his jeans was getting wet and scrambled up into a squatting position.

"Anyway," Geordie said, "I didn't want to go to school today. That's why I'm here now."

Billy shrugged. "What's the time?"

11

Geordie looked at his watch. "Three thirty-three and fifty-seven, fifty-eight secs, fifty-nine, three thirty-four and one..."

"All right," Billy grunted. "I still wouldn't swap it for a good dog. Quarter of an hour." It took twenty-five minutes to get down to Davieburn. The school bus reached the village at quarter past four. If they went back along the line of the old railway no one would see them until they were right in the middle of the village; then it would look as though Geordie was on his way home from the bus-stop. It was just Geordie who didn't want to be seen, Billy wasn't worried about himself.

"Peter Ward'll be up in his hut by now," Billy said, gazing towards the gradual slopes on the left side of Craigmore Hill, across the valley. People always thought of Peter Ward when they looked at the wild part of the hill. "He's always there by March."

"What's that smoke?" said Geordie suddenly.

A gout of black smoke had just pushed itself up from among the grey of trees below the steeper, right-hand edge of Craigmore. For a moment it paused and gathered, like a giant black fist shaken over the Davieburn Vale, a fist attached to the earth by a black forearm knotted with muscles of smoke; then it extended, swiftly, crawling up the sky.

"Is it...?" Geordie muttered.

It intensified and spread, cloud upon cloud billowing up now, towering into the still clean air.

"It's the Yard," Billy said, getting up.

Both boys watched anxiously. The smoke was so sudden and so black. It was like a reminder that it was Davieburn Vale, not Culane Hill, where they lived their lives – that that was their world, that things happened there and troubles were not imaginary.

"I know what it is," said Geordie at last. "It's that polystyrene. Dad said he was going to set light to it."

"Dod Moffat told my dad he'd sue us if he did that."

"Dod Moffat? Why?"

"He said the smoke would poison his beasts."

"It's not blowing his way," Geordie said. "It's not doing him any harm."

"That's what he said," Billy answered grimly. He hated the thought of a feud developing between his people and the old farmer. "Your dad's an idiot," he hissed at Geordie, savagely. "He's just an idiot, that's all he is. My dad says that stuff never needed burned."

"It was getting blown about," Geordie countered. "It was getting into the trees and onto the fields. Dod Moffat's cows might have eaten it, and then what would have happened?"

"Come on, let's go," Billy said. He left the summit of the hill, leaping in giant strides down the steep bank of the Cairn.

Geordie hurried down after him. "We'll be too early. We'll be caught," he said.

"You can stay here then," Billy snapped back. "I'm not caring."

Geordie followed. They went in silence, Billy always a few steps ahead, while the path became a well-trodden track, then a hard stony track and then, past two steel posts with red-painted tops, a narrow tarred road. They passed the first house, an old stone cottage surrounded by a fuchsia hedge, and were soon between the russet beech-hedges of the road down to Davieburn.

"Tell your mum you got a lift back with Dave Simmers, and I'll tell mine the same," said Billy. Dave Simmers always drove past the school on a Tuesday as everyone was coming out. Sometimes he would give one of the girls a lift.

"She'd never believe me," Geordie said, with scorn.

"Then tell her she shouldn't ask questions if she's not going to believe the answers."

Billy's father was back late. Billy and his mother and Rob and Liz had finished their supper by the time he got in. Rob hobbled out to feed his greyhound.

Billy's father washed. Not that it made a great deal of difference: his face and hands were more or less permanently ingrained with black oil, except for when he used his special cleaning mixture at the end of the week. The grime accentuated the piercing blue of his eyes: they were steel-blue, sapphire-blue, like sapphires set in jet. But tonight his blue eyes were clouded.

He had been out with the lorry all afternoon. When he had come back to the Yard with a load of scrap, he had found Andy Gibbon and Dod Moffat in the middle of a shouting match. Dod Moffat had called Andy Gibbon a dirty little rat.

A weight of apprehension settled over Billy. The incident was like the usual village talk in some ways: you listened with half an ear, there was nothing really out of the ordinary about it. In itself, it hardly seemed enough to explain the gloom that slowly filled his mind.

Andy Gibbon had waited until Billy's father was gone that afternoon before he had set light to the huge mound of polystyrene dumped on the tip. There was nothing peculiar about that: Andy Gibbon and Will Stuart were partners, they each took decisions. It wasn't as if Andy Gibbon had done it behind Will Stuart's back. And yet...

Billy knew something was wrong up at the Yard, he knew it in his bones: something

15

hidden under the surface.

Dod Moffat had been hopping mad. He had come straight over and insisted on them putting out the fire at once, or he'd call the Fire Brigade. There was an old pressure-hose at the Yard. Andy Gibbon and the two other lads who worked there had taken over an hour to dampen down the flames, choking and coughing in the poisonous black reek. Dod Moffat had returned to give Andy a further piece of his mind. That was how Billy's father had found them.

Will Stuart pursed his lips. "He said he regretted the day he ever sold us the land for the Yard" – he was imitating the old farmer's officious style – "and if he had any further cause for complaint against us, he'd call the police."

"Well, let him!" Billy's mother was ready for battle. "The Tip belongs to the Yard, not him. He's just opening his big mouth."

Billy's father fell silent. Billy's mother rumbled dishes noisily in the sink. Liz went to the mirror and began to brush her hair. So Billy was the only one who heard his father muttering into his cup of tea: "I'm not wanting the police coming in about the Yard."

Billy's heart froze. It was something about his voice. He got up from the kitchen table and went through the open door into the living-room, switched on the television. There was

16

nothing much on: it was just for something to do.

Of course, no one wanted the police calling by like that anyway. Billy remembered the famous story about the taxman calling at the Yard, when he found no one there because they'd all gone and hidden in the bushes. People still laughed about that time now, down at the Bridge Bar.

But there was something different here. There was no laughter. It almost seemed to Billy as though his father was trying not to be frightened. It wasn't like him.

And now he was trying to sound jaunty. "Anyway, Andy wasn't over-worried about the stuff," he said. "He said it might come in useful sometime. True enough, I suppose."

"What would that stuff come in useful for?" his mother retorted scornfully.

"I don't know. Packing, maybe."

His mother snorted.

Rob came back in. "I'm needing the vet again," he said. "Her foot's none better. I'll go in the morning."

"Are you not working tomorrow?" their mother asked.

Rob grunted. Like many of the men in Davieburn, Billy's brother Rob worked at the big glassworks six miles down the road. Like most of them, he never missed an opportunity of taking a day off. But the greyhound, who was a regular winner at local races, was worth a lot of money to him anyway. Her foot had been poisoned for almost a week. For that week Rob and his greyhound had limped around together, the tall brindled bitch elegant even on her three legs, Rob dragging his wasted leg and deep-soled boot just as he had done for fifteen years.

Billy liked the greyhound well enough. She would nuzzle his hand, thrusting her long satin head up past his wrist. But she was Rob's dog; she was almost like a part of Rob, the part of him that had never run or leaped or danced. Rob only ever talked about how much she was worth, but Billy had a vague feeling that when he talked about her value in money he was actually meaning something else – like how much he loved her, perhaps. Everyone Billy knew talked about money – even Geordie, even Dod Moffat. But there was something in Billy that seemed to stand back from it, like a foreigner who didn't know the language: he had no real idea of the value of money.

At nine o'clock the news came on the TV, and Billy went out of the living-room. He went to his bedroom and looked out of the window. You could still see out through an arch-shaped bit at the top, but all the lower part of the glass had a fur of frost over it. Billy and Rob's bedroom was at the back of the house; it looked out over the neighbouring farmer's fields, and there were no street lights. There were hard bright stars in a black sky.

The weight grew in Billy's mind. If his mother and Liz had heard what his father muttered it might have been different. But only he had heard it: and something warned him that he had been entrusted with an awful secret.

He scratched a car in the frost on the window. He scratched a small dome on top of the car, and lines coming out of the dome: a car with a flashing light on the top. He scratched FUZZ along the side of the car.

Then, almost automatically, his finger began to trace something else. To begin with it looked like the silhouette of Culane Hill; but as his nail moved over the glass, it turned into a head. The muzzle; and two bumps on the head for ears. The head was side-on, looking this way. The ears were half-raised, but turned over softly out to the sides. The warmth of his forefinger melted a pit-like eye; a quarter-moon scratch was the other one. But it was not in the eye that the dog's expression lay, but in the turn of its head – slightly towards him, but as if it could see other things all around as well, and was watching out warily for him. Not a greyhound's head, built for speed and splitting the air like an arrow; but a strong head, a strong stubbed muzzle, a wide wise forehead between the eyes. And now, thick coarse hair at the neck, and a broad chest, and a front leg,

19

elbow drawn up well beside the chest, the paw raised. And the back in a steady incline down to the bottom of the window. The dog was standing on a hill, facing uphill, looking around in the starlight for danger, but it had just turned its head to look at Billy, to let him know that it was there. It was so real Billy could almost feel the rank warmth of its hair. Not a dog built and bred for racing with other dogs on a cramped course while men looked on breathlessly – nothing like that, nothing to do with money: a dog for wide open hillsides, for scanning horizons, for running through the snow and broken yellow grass and heather, a dog with thick coarse hair and thousand-year-old eyes, Dog as he had been for thousands and millions of years, running with the hunters, running for the herdsmen, sitting with the chiefs and the kings with red tongue lolling and white teeth gleaming.

Billy suddenly felt that they'd soon sort the police out, if they came to the Yard. And when they'd sorted the police out, they'd soon sort out what was hidden up there, what was wrong. Why Dad never talked, and why Dod Moffat hated Andy Gibbon so...

Billy had eaten a huge supper. Since half past eight that morning he had been out on the hills with Geordie. They must have walked or run fifteen or twenty miles, and nothing at dinner-time. He straightened up from the window. The frost had already filmed over the police car again, but the Dog was still clear. Billy undressed, left his clothes on the floor, put on his pyjamas and flopped into bed without putting the light on or drawing the curtains. He felt cold and so did the bed, but he was asleep in minutes.

Package 2

Hobart, Tasmania
May 1, 1984

Dear Roger,

Well, first of all I suppose I should
say I'm surprised you liked Chapter
One. Glad, of course, but surprised. No
reason, really – I mean, I didn't think
it was *that* bad: just doubted that anything I'd written could be OK, by you
or by anyone else…

   The criticism: well, my first reac-
tion when you say things like you "want
to know who it is that's telling the
story" is to say: obviously, me –
idiot! Who else? Theresa Thain, you
know me, remember? Friends for eight
years plus. OK, you meant something
more subtle than that. However, I still
don't think I should have included
myself in the Story. How could I have
done, except by saying something like:
"I used to know this boy Billy Stuart
ten years ago and this is his story"?
Honestly, I wasn't any part of it. I'll
include myself in the one or two little

bits where I did come into it, but
that's all. I only really became part
of it once the real bit - the bit
that's going to be the Story - was
over.

At the same time I feel, in some
peculiar way, that you do have a point.
In fact, reading over the diary that I
kept back then, I see it's really quite
a big point.

So I've thought about it a lot, and
I've come to a decision. It's a bit of
a wrench, but I'm going to send you the
diary I kept back then. From October
1973, that is. The Story - Billy's
story - begins in March 1973 and finishes, I suppose, in the August. At
least, that's when it stopped being the
story of Billy alone - when he was
recovering after the accident. In the
September we were starting to get to
know each other properly; and then the
Diary starts after that.

However, I'm not going to send you
the diary all together: I'm going to
send it to you in bits. That may seem
cock-eyed, but I have my reasons. What
I'll do is, I'll send you each chapter
of the Story as I write it and then
make the weight of the package up with
a bit of the Diary - I want to get my

money's worth from the postage, with
the price it is. It does mean ripping
the diary to bits, which *is* hard, but –
what the hell, it isn't doing anything
here. That's one reason. The other
reason is – well, what? I want you to
see them happening together, the diary
from ten years ago and the story from
eleven years ago: two separate stories
which both really finish up at the same
point. The story of what happened, and
the story of how we found out what happened, Billy Stuart and I – how we
found out what had been forgotten.
Billy's story and my story, woven
together, the way they should be.

One other thing: I don't want you to
make any more comments in between chapters, because that'll put me off, and
I'll probably stop writing it altogether, and then you'll spend the rest
of your life dying of curiosity.

In fact, you've put me off already,
which is why I'm sending you only the
first bit of the diary just now, and
none of the story. (Actually it's
because I haven't quite finished Chapter Two yet.)

As ever,
Theresa

DIARY

October 22nd, 1973

I'm scared to sleep. That's why I'm writing this. I've decided I'm going to be completely honest in this diary. I've tried being honest with people in real life, but it doesn't work, so I'm going to be honest here.

Does that mean writing down my dreams as well? I want to get away from them. I mean, I don't want to get away from them exactly, I just want to know why they keep coming. I'd be better writing this in the day-time, I wouldn't so much mind writing my dreams down when it's light. But then what would I do at night? I'd just lie awake and think and think, and my heart would start thumping and I'd get that sweaty feeling in my hands and that prickling in my neck.

Maybe I should tell Billy about the dreams – I've never really wanted to. But I do like him so much; he's so sort of – quiet, and he listens to me when I jibber on. I don't understand how he can be so – different, in the dreams.

They're not exactly memories – the dreams, I mean. I know that because then – on the actual night – I didn't actually see him coming along the track to the house, and that's what he's doing in the dreams – most often it's the bit between those low walls on the way out of the farm close. I only saw him when he came to the door, and of course he was just walking, not floating. And the thing is, when it happened, on the night, when he came here, and into the kitchen, and we'd got over our fright at being woken up by him, and the state he was in – I just felt sorry for him: well, I wanted to hold him and make him better, I suppose I wanted to mother him. Or something! What I'm trying to say is, there was nothing scary about him; he'd blood all over his face, of course, and his hair was full of blood too, and he was all pale – shocked, I suppose. In fact he was shattered. But he was all right – he was still Billy. I didn't know that then, but since I've got to know him properly I can see, looking back, that he was just the ordinary Billy that night.

But in the dreams – I don't know... What makes it so horrible is that he seems to *like* looking that way, in the dreams. I mean, he knows what he looks like – he's sort of *aware*. And he wants to look like that. And that's why he floats above the ground – just, I don't know, as high as my knee above the ground. And he doesn't have any expression on his face, but somehow you know he's laughing at you. He's sneering.

26

The other night, the blood wasn't just anyhow over his face: it was, like, in a mask, it was a sort of pattern round his eyes and mouth: his eyes and his mouth were like three black holes in the blood, gaping at me. It's not always like that.

I didn't want to write about that. I wish I hadn't.

What else can I write about? No one talks to Billy about what happened in the summer. Even the newspaper men and the police didn't get anything out of him. Mum says an experience like that can affect your character really, really deeply. She says it can leave a scar on your personality that never heals. So he doesn't talk about it, nor does anyone else. No one else knows about the business with Drift either – except his parents. He's told me a bit about it, how it affected him and that. I think I would have been completely broken by it. That was all happening right at the start – I mean, when I first got to know him, nearly six months ago now. I thought he'd got off the bus to speak to me, but in fact it was all because of Drift.

I want to go back, I must get myself in order. I want to write a book about Billy, but I don't know where to start. I could start with a diary, that's what I thought when I started writing this. I can't really think where to start though. Mum wouldn't approve of

me spending so much attention on Billy. I
know she doesn't approve of him. When he
came here that night after the accident, she
was OK with him then, in fact she was really
nice – but that was just because he was a
Fellow Creature in Distress. And it was even
her that suggested I should go over and visit
him when he was recovering. Dad was really
strange about Drift.

I've not told Mum that Billy's asked me to
go to Bucksburn with him on Friday night.
She's sure to make a fuss. That's another big
worry.

Right, it's only two o' clock. I'm going to
write for another hour, then I'm going to go
to bed. I don't care if I don't sleep.

It's the end of October now, that makes it
six months. My very first confrontation with
Billy Stuart must have been at the end of
April. It was that stupid day when he got off
the bus at my stop, and I thought he wanted
to speak to me. I couldn't think what else he
could have got off for, I mean, it's a completely empty road. Apart from our farm
road, and there's no other house near. I
didn't know about Drift. He just mumbled
something at me and then walked off. I
didn't know what to think. I thought he must
have wanted to ask me out, and then taken
fright! And then he disappeared down onto
the old railway track and I was left feeling

like a real dummy because I'd smiled at him.
I suppose I must have been trying to encourage him.

It seems so long ago. You feel like a completely different person after six months,
you've grown up so much. But sometimes
you can feel like a completely different
person after a week as well. But sometimes I
think there's a part of you that's sort of looking down on yourself as you grow up, and
that part of you's hundreds and hundreds of
years old, and knows it all already. So that
when something new happens to you, when
you experience something that makes you
grow up a bit more, that other you that's sort
of looking down just nods and says, yes, I
know all that. And then the real you that's
down below, that's fourteen or fifteen or
whatever, nods, too, and feels she's just recognized something again – it's not really
new, she's done it before.

Anyway, I did encourage Billy after that. I
felt right stupid sometimes. I would grin all
over my face whenever I saw him. Once I
was eating an ice-cream and I forgot about it
when I smiled at him, and then I realized I
had ice-cream all down my chin. What a
sight! I don't think he knew what had hit
him. Actually, I couldn't help it. Whenever I
saw him, I just grinned like an imbecile.

I found out where he went at the weekends, what sort of things he did. The bike-run down the side of the big Bing and all that. That was through Geordie. But I didn't really meet him, face to face to talk to, until that time in July, during the holidays, when I sort of cycled over in Davieburn direction, and sort of accidentally bumped into him. He was alone then. At that time he wasn't going about with any of his friends, not even Geordie. All because of Drift. I really like Geordie still – no, I'm going to write about that another time.

So, I met him for the second time. I engineered a meeting. He was really morose. But I thought, well, if he doesn't like my company, there's nothing keeping him, he doesn't have to stay and talk to me. I can't even remember how I started talking: I must have suddenly turned into an amazing conversationalist. I don't like it at the big Bing, I don't like the smell of it, and all the bushes and weeds look sort of spindly and all the wrong colour. I suppose that's the farmer's daughter in me coming out. You look at all that huge heap of stuff that's come out from inside the earth, and it looks so horrible and sort of barren, just grey and waste, and you think, nothing'll ever grow on it, not properly – it'll never become a real hill, like Culane or Craigmore, with sheep and rabbits and stuff. So that's what I said to him – well, more or less – well,

not in so many words: what I just said was,
Do you like it here? He was just sitting there,
scraping the shale and stuff around with his
foot, and he said, It's all right.

That's right. Then I saw some raspberries
on the other side of the path and I started to
pick them. They weren't very good. I said,
Do you want one? and he said no, he didn't
like them. I had on my Marc Bolan T-shirt
and he said, Where did you get that T-shirt? I
told him how I'd sent away for it. So I asked
him if he liked T Rex and he said he didn't
like any music. I said, Why not? and he just
shrugged. Then he said discos and all that
were shite. I wonder if I should put words
like that in my diary. Well, I said I was going
to be honest. Maybe it's all right for the
diary but not the Book. I was really glad
Jemma wasn't with me because I know we'd
just have giggled and been stupid and I'm
sure he'd have been put off. I said I liked
discos but I hardly ever got to any. He said
his sister went to one in Falkirk every week,
she got all this stupid gear on and tried to
look sexy and put all this stuff on her face
and stank of perfume. I said I didn't do that,
though sometimes I put a bit of eyeliner on.
And he said, Why? and I said because it
makes your eyes look nicer. And then he suddenly looked me in the eyes, and I – well, I
went all funny inside. I felt like my whole

stomach was dropping away. He looked
really scruffy, and his hair was all falling
over his face and it looked as though it
needed a good wash. But he's got these blue
eyes – a really sort of deep, piercing blue, and
the way he looked at me was so sudden and
unexpected... I was telling myself, he's really
just a dirty little boy, but I couldn't get his
eyes out of my mind – it was as if they'd got
right inside me. I just said to him, I'll maybe
see you another time; and got on my bike
again. I said, The summer holidays are really
boring, aren't they? and he grunted something and picked up a stone and threw it
somewhere. Then I said I would lend him
some of my T Rex records so that he could
listen to them properly because I was sure
he'd like them – I wasn't really, but that's
what I said. I hate T Rex now, that's because
of his influence. He's got really definite taste
in music now. He likes real Underground
stuff, some of it's dead weird – Yes and the
Doors and that. And he said all right, so I
said I'd bring them next time I was coming
this way. But then all the trouble happened –
Grandad and the Accident and everything –
and we both forgot about music for a bit.

Package 3

Hobart
May 13, 1984

Dear Roger,

Chapter Two – at last!
  I know it's a bit weird – but you
asked for it: you wanted to know who's
telling the story, so you got it! A
stupid thing to want, if you ask me,
but it certainly got me thinking.
  I never said I'd be sending the bits
of the diary that were connected with
the particular chapters of the story –
I'm just ripping a few pages out of the
diary each time I send you a chapter of
the story. There's none of it really
connected, anyway: it was two different
seasons – spring into summer, autumn
into winter – almost like two different
worlds. I'm struck, as I write this, by
how strange it is sitting here in May
and it's actually the start of winter.
  Anyway, I just wanted to say that I
really do appreciate having you there
on tenterhooks waiting for the next
episode – it really keeps me going. And

Billy's Drift

I can assure you, I really do need
something to keep me going through the
Tasmanian winter. It's as bad as Scotland, only without the advantage of
being Home. I feel more and more about
my little story that it's like a candle
to light me through the dark, wet
nights. I hurry home in the evenings
and rush through my various chores so I
can sit down to my hour of scribbling,
crossing out, typing up, re-typing…

Now, stop writing letters to me about
it, will you?

T.T.

DIARY

October 23rd, 1973

I wrote an amazing lot last night. But I couldn't wake up this morning. I fell asleep at breakfast, and Mum let me go back to bed and take the day off school. She said I didn't look right. I was really glad, it's a really horrible day, sleet and wind and everything. I must stop saying "really" all the time.

I just can't write during the day. I tried this afternoon, but it wouldn't work. I've started to look forward to night-time already, when I can write.

I must tell Mum about Bucksburn, tomorrow. Somehow I've got to bring myself to do it.

Billy's only ever been here twice, once about Drift, and once the time after the Accident. I've been at his house eleven times. Mum's only known about three: the other times I told her I was with Jemma. Billy's mother's fine, she doesn't bother about anything. She refers to me as "Billy's girlfriend", and they treat me just like one of the family. Girlfriend! He's never even touched me – well, not *properly*.

It was weird, the way he suddenly said, do you want to go to Bucksburn? This was last week – Friday, I suppose. I said, all right, but

why Bucksburn? I just thought, he said. Then
I realized he probably doesn't want to go
where the other ones from school were. Then
I thought, does that mean he doesn't want to
be seen with me? But then he doesn't mind
being seen with me at school. So I thought he
doesn't want any of the ones from the school
seeing him dancing, because he probably
thinks he can't. A lot of boys think they can't
dance, so they make themselves go all stiff
and stupid, and then they really can't. It's all
right to say "really" there. But I wouldn't
make him dance if he didn't want to. I've
never been to the disco in Bucksburn. I only
went to the one in Blackhall that once, and
Mum only allowed me because Sam was
home on his holidays and would take me,
and she made him promise not to let me out
of his sight. I'm sure it'd be a better way of
breaking Mum in if I asked to go to the
Blackhall disco first with Billy. She probably
thinks Bucksburn's the other side of the
world, or a seething den of iniquity or something. I wonder why Billy really wants to go
there. I wonder if it's got something to do
with You-know-what.

Maybe I should choose my moment when I
ask her. Maybe I should do it when Dad's
there. I never really know about Dad. Sometimes I think he'll be on my side, but I'm not
really sure.

October 24th, 1973

I asked her. About Bucksburn, I mean. I
decided to get her alone, and in a good
mood. I didn't want Dad there. I was really
helpful first, and I was helping her dry the
dishes after supper – I'd been going to say I'd
do all the dishes, clear them up and wash
them and dry them, but I thought she might
get suspicious and think I was trying to get
something out of her. I probably did it the
wrong way. You've probably got to have a
ten-year degree in Psychology before you
learn to handle your mum. I said that a lot of
the girls in my class went to Bucksburn
sometimes because there was a good disco
there that was for younger folk and – and
that's as far as I got. She said, Well, I'm not
letting you go. I said, oh, Mum – just once,
I'm just going with Jemma, she says it's really
good, or something like that. A bit obvious,
really. Mum just looked at me and – oh, hell!
I knew she could see right through me.

I don't feel like writing tonight. I went into
my bedroom, and I've been here ever since. I
thumped my head against the wall till it hurt.
Well, a bit. I didn't want to do it too hard in
case it loosened my brain or something. Oh,
why does she have to be like that? I'm fifteen
next month, and she still wants to treat me
like a child! Why doesn't anyone else have a

37

problem like this with their mother?

She went mad. She just stood there yelling at me. Well, she didn't really, I suppose, not until I started yelling at her. I suppose I'm going to have to apologize to her, or there'll be a horrible atmosphere in the house for days. It's not fair, why does it always have to be me? Well, I'm not going to apologize tonight anyway.

Or tomorrow, either.

October 27th, 1973

There was a film on TV about someone who had amnesia. I thought it was just like Billy. This man had witnessed a murder, years before, and it had been too awful, so he'd just blanked it out. But after a while he started having bad dreams. Oh, God, I've just thought of something terrible... No, it can't be right, I'm not even going to write it down. Everyone said it was an accident. The police, too. But it must have been bad enough for Billy anyway.

He was great about Bucksburn. I felt really stupid telling him I wasn't allowed to go. His mum lets him go anywhere he wants. She moans at him but she still lets him go. I wonder if that's because he's a boy. No, it's not, I think it's *class*. Mum's just a snob. She thinks I'd get mixed up with roughs and the Working Classes. She'd never admit that – she'd just say there's nothing wrong with working people whatsoever and when's she ever objected to Tam and Alex coming to have their dinner in the kitchen with everyone else when they're working here. But with her own dear little daughter it'd be a different matter altogether. Deep down, she's an awful snob. That's why she doesn't like Billy. Just because he lives in a council house.

Everyone's tried to jog his memory by telling him the bits they do know, but he just can't seem to relate it to anything he remembers. I said, did he remember being shut up or stuck anywhere? He looked really strange for a moment, and then he said something like, When you say that – this is what he said – I get a sort of picture in my mind, like I'm shut up in a shed, and I must be lying on the floor because I'm looking out under the door. But the door's not up to much – he meant it wasn't a very strong-looking door. He couldn't think why he wouldn't just shove it and go out. But then he said he was sure none of that was real. Then there's the baler-twine. On the night of the accident, his hands and feet were tied with baler-twine – I know they were, because he showed us the marks on his wrists. But he wasn't tied up when he came to the house, and a week afterwards he said he didn't remember anything about being tied up. There's another thing he says he remembers: white birds, a sort of door opening and white birds flying up into the trees. But he said that couldn't be real either. When I asked him why not he said, I don't know. He always finishes by saying that.

It's really strange to think that that's going on inside him. I think I know him quite well now. I know what makes him laugh, and I know when he's going to get cross about something, and when he's sulky. I mean, maybe you can never really get into someone else and get to know them *properly*, but I think I know him quite well. He's sort of firm: he keeps his mind on one thing when mine's jumping about all over the place. I feel *I've* got the disintegrating personality, he always seems to be so all there. So how is it that something's keeping his whole mind in some sort of prison?

It gets really scary sitting here writing like this. I've got my thick socks on and my woolly dressing-gown over my pyjamas, and the fire's on too, but I still feel all chilly up my back. Maybe it's when I think it's late at night and everything's so huge and dark outside. There's miles and miles of black land out there, fields and woods and bings and hills and ditches, and no one out in it and no lights, and it feels – yeugh. It makes me go all shuddery. I keep my light on all the time now. Mum grumbles a bit about the electricity, but Dad says lights don't burn much really. Maybe I should have tried to get Dad to help about Bucksburn.

CHAPTER
2

THE BRIDGE

"I was never allowed to go out at your age." Billy's mother was harassed, what with having to wash the dishes by herself, and her curlers still in and the bus leaving in half an hour. "If my mother had caught me with lipstick on, my, she'd have thrashed me to an inch of my life."

"So when did she let you out?" Liz's voice was preoccupied, almost calm: she was looking for her other white shoe.

"Not for a long time yet." Billy's mother took her headscarf off and tugged at her first curler pin. "When I was your age, I was doing the laundry for the whole street, not doing myself up like goodness-knows-what every other night."

"Well—" The temperature was rising: Liz had found her shoe and paused a moment as her foot wriggled into it. "If you were married

42

at eighteen, you must have been awful busy for a few months if you really had as many boyfriends as you let on. Or maybe you had them all *after* you married Dad!" She ducked behind her mother and flounced out of the kitchen. Billy heard the front door slam a minute later.

He looked up: he was amazed at her daring. That was strong, even for Liz! His mother was muttering in front of the mirror, a furious flush across her cheek.

If anyone had asked Billy what he knew about women, he would have replied that they quarrelled a lot. That seemed to be the only thing about them that was worth considering.

It was Saturday. Liz had her disco, his mother had her bingo, his father went to the Bridge Bar and Billy and Rob went with him. Liz got her bus in one direction, his mother got hers in the other. At eight o'clock Billy and his father got into the van and set off for the Bridge. Rob had been there since opening time.

There was no pub in Davieburn itself, but a couple of miles from anywhere else, close to the old bridge over the Davieburn, there was an old house that had been turned into a hotel. The Bridge Bar was a modern, flat-roofed extension at one end of it, and people came to it from miles around, especially at weekends. There was, in sharp contrast, another extension at the opposite end of the old building: it was a rather high-class restaurant, and the local people used it seldom – perhaps occasionally a farmer after a particularly successful market.

It was dark. They took the long way round, past the Bing. The Avenue was the more direct road, but it was narrow and its twists and turns made it slower to drive on. The black mass of the Bing passed them on their right. Billy and Geordie and their friends had been there all that afternoon, making a dangerous steep run for their bikes. Billy was bruised all over, his nails were torn and his sandshoe heels were in tatters.

In the car park outside the bar were Dod Moffat's battered ex-Post Office van, Andy Gibbon's BMW, Dave Simmers' large, well-polished white van, and half a dozen others. Most people thought nothing of the walk. Will Stuart parked in his usual rut in the hard-core and they went in, parting as usual at the door. Billy's father made his way through the crowd, pausing every now and then for a greeting and a few words; Billy, avoiding the crowd, went to the fruit machine.

It was the old-fashioned type of fruit machine: varnished plywood; a display of nine fruits, three by three; three hold buttons and the start button; no gimmickry or flashing lights or flashy artwork. A sign above the buttons said: NOT TO BE PLAYED BY PERSONS UNDER EIGHTEEN YEARS. The machine bored Billy, bored him stupid, but it was one of those things like school: it was just there – you went to school on the weekdays and on Saturday evenings you played the fruit machine. Because it was there. Billy would play it from quarter past eight to eleven o'clock.

Press. Orange, plum and melon. Press and rock, just slightly. Orange, plum and plum. Hold, and press again. Three plums: *tick, tick, tick, tick, tick*, a clatter of coins into the tray. Billy picked a five pence piece out and put it into the slot to start again.

He knew the machine inside out. He had no idea how he knew, he just knew. It was almost like a part of him. He never thought about it, he just let his mind wander. He didn't always win, but he always knew, the moment he had pressed, when he wasn't going to win anything. If his father gave him fifty pence as pocket money, he would always have a pound anyway by the end of the night. Yet he didn't play for money, but out of boredom.

Everywhere around, people were drinking and talking loudly. Men with red faces pushing through with their tray of drinks to where wives or girlfriends sat at the window-tables, legs crossed, cigarettes between red-nailed fingers. A clear space in the air just above the drinkers, then about two feet above their

45

heads blue smoke thickening towards the ceiling – three distinct layers: heads, air and smoke. The two lads from the Yard, in open-necked shirts even in the raw of early spring, their sleeves rolled up over their hairy arms. Dod Moffat hunched at a corner of the bar, like a stone that's sat by a riverside for ten thousand years. Billy's father was speaking to him. Dod Moffat's face remained impassive as it always did, the wide flat nose with the large wart beside it, the broad compressed line of his mouth, the massive jaws clenching and unclenching as if he were chewing his whisky: always the same, from minute to minute and from month to month. Occasionally he would lift his flat grey cap as if to let some air in around the smooth, bald dome underneath; occasionally he would flare his nostrils and pick his nose with a black, broken nail: but no movement he made could alter his expression. Seeing them together, Dod Moffat with his immobility, Will Stuart with his animated gestures, was like watching someone kicking a football against a wall, yet there was still the ghost of a similarity between the two men: both had farming in their ancestry. Billy wondered if they were trying to make amends for last Tuesday's row. Andy Gibbon was at the far end of the bar, and Billy's father occasionally glanced towards him.

Billy became aware of someone behind him,

looking over his shoulder. Someone tall, with a lounging way about him. He didn't bother to look round, he knew it was Dave Simmers. He knew it was Dave Simmers by the pricking feeling in the back of his neck.

It was not as though Billy had anything definite against Dave Simmers. It was just that, if ever Dave Simmers came and stood behind him like that, it felt as though someone was holding out a bare high-voltage wire which at any moment might touch your skin. Billy's back tingled all over.

"Any hens, Davie?" someone said softly. Still Billy kept his head towards the fruit machine.

"How many?" Dave Simmers' voice.

"Twenty?"

"A tenner."

"That'll do. When can you get them to me?"

"Next Wednesday, maybe. I'll drop them by."

There was a growing number of white hens in the neighbourhood, all supplied by Dave Simmers. No one knew exactly what the arrangement was, but Dave Simmers' brother worked with battery hens at a factory near Bucksburn, and the supply of hens seemed to be unlimited. Most people saw it as a well-earned release for the birds – poor pale, half-feathered things that had never seen the sun or grass, but within a month would be full-bodied and glossy, pecking and raking as joyously as any farm-bred fowl – and so no questions were asked.

But however the conversation behind him went, Billy knew that Dave Simmers' mind was really on the fruit machine, that he was sick with envy at what Billy could get out of it. But watch as he might, he had never been able to learn the knack that Billy had with it – if it could be learned. Feeling him there, watching, Billy for a moment or two almost felt an interest in what he was doing. Press. Hold, nudge. Three plums. *Tick, tick, tick, tick, tick.* Fifty pence.

The evening wore on. The red-faced men grew redder. Billy's father's eyes grew bluer as his pupils contracted into points. He seemed to be hanging onto the bar with one hand, while his other clutched his whisky glass. Billy judged he would be another quarter of an hour. He was talking to one of the red-faced men: a tall, weather-scarred man, plainly another farmer a little ill at ease in his sports jacket and collar and tie. Billy couldn't remember seeing him before or put a name to him. The man looked over in Billy's direction a few times as they talked; Billy's father did the same, but was unable to focus. Billy wondered why they kept looking at him. He left the machine and went to the toilet.

As he came back he heard a crash. He saw

his father had fallen off his stool and was lying on the floor. The red-faced farmer and somebody else heaved him up by the armpits, and Rob appeared from somewhere to help. It was time to go. Rob pulled his father's left arm round his neck and over his shoulder. Billy got under the right arm. Rob had most of the weight. Billy felt his father take a deep breath, and knew he was going to sing.

Sing he did. "More, much more than this," he roared, "I did it my-y-y-y way..." On steadier nights he would sing the whole song; when the drink had got on top of him it was just the chorus. He stumbled sideways, and Billy got the full weight of him, jarring him all down his back. He tried to get a tighter grip of the huge muscle of his father's forearm. The drinkers parted to let them through, and someone opened the door for them.

"I'll run you back, Will," a voice said. It was Andy Gibbon. Billy wasn't sure that he looked much fitter than his father.

"Get away!" his father sang. "I'm the driver!"

"Come on, don't be stupid. I'll take you back in my motor." Billy decided he must be sober after all, though his face was very red and bleary.

"In *your* motor?" His father stopped dead in his tracks, jerking Billy and Rob with him. "In your motor? What would I be doing in

49

your motor?" He sounded as though Andy Gibbon had just suggested flying to the moon. "What's wrong with *my* van?"

"Come on, man, don't be stupid," Andy Gibbon said again. "You can get your motor again tomorrow. I'm not going to drive it back and then have to come back here for my car."

"Oh, I see," Billy's father said, wagging his head up and down and mincing his words carefully, laying on the irony. "My van's not good enough, that's what it is. You'd not be seen dead in my van, that's what it is. You'd not be seen dead in anything less than a BMW – pardon me for forgetting."

"What's gotten into you, Will?" Andy Gibbon looked genuinely hurt. "Come on, man, I've driven you home before."

But Billy's father lurched forward determinedly. Rob and Billy kept quiet. It was not their argument. Billy heard his father muttering, "He'd drive a man to drink, so he would." Andy Gibbon was left standing where he had been in the middle of the car park, the lights of the Bridge Bar reflected in a puddle at his feet.

The brothers had to slot their father through the van door and put in the ignition keys for him. But once in the driver's seat Will Stuart became a different man. He started up with complete assurance, and, weaving in and out of the parked cars, except for forgetting to switch on the headlights, might have been taken for a perfectly proficient driver. He said nothing, either about the conversation with Andy Gibbon or about anything else.

Billy was puzzled himself about what his father had been saying, but in his gut he agreed with him. His father and Andy Gibbon were partners in business: how was it then that everything Andy Gibbon had was newer, better, more expensive than everything the Stuarts had?

They were home. Another Saturday night over, a Saturday night much like a hundred others Billy could remember. Geordie Gibbon had to go to church every Sunday: his mother was very religious and wanted Geordie to have as good an upbringing as she had had. Billy didn't have to go to church, but he had to go to the pub every Saturday night: it was just a thing you accepted. At least you didn't have to get dressed up to go to the pub.

It had started to rain, and Beth Stuart's make-up would have run by the time she got back from the bus-stop and found her man snoring.

Package 4

Hobart

Dear Roger,

I keep going, it keeps coming. Here's
Chapter 3, right on schedule.

T.T.

DIARY

January 5th, 1974

I had a really good talk with Dad last night.
I'm definitely going to make sure he's there
this time when I ask about Bucksburn. I
forgot, I haven't written about Bucksburn.
It's so long since I kept my Diary. I was
sleeping so well for such a long time, I must
have been exhausted! And then there was
Christmas, and it was all lovely. The snow
started at ten o'clock on Christmas Eve, and
it's only just going away properly now.
Ronnie and Sam were both home this year,
just for Christmas though, not for New Year.
Of course Ronnie wasn't here half an hour
before he and Dad were quarrelling. About
rape! I was trying to imagine what the argument would have meant if it had been about
sex and not about feeding sheep. I'll write
about Bucksburn in a moment.

Happy New Year, everyone! I keep forgetting this is a private diary.

I think Dad hasn't quite recovered from
Hogmanay yet, that's why he's been sitting
about so much in the last few days. Of
course this was the first New Year we didn't
get a visit from Grandad, and Granny didn't
want to come by herself. It was really sad, I

enjoyed his visits – so did Dad. Mum's really
relieved of course. She hated it when he came
– you could see she was itching to go around
after him with a brush and a bottle of disin-
fectant, and she could never get him out of
the house quick enough. Grandad was fifty
when Mum was born: Dad says it was a big
age gap and she and Grandad never got a
chance to be close. Mum's forty-seven, which
means Grandad must have been 97! I think
that's amazing. It was an incredible funeral,
more like a public holiday – there seemed to
be thousands of people.

I'm too tired to write about Bucksburn
tonight.

January 7th, 1974

Isn't it typical! The bad dreams have started
again. It's almost as if it's to do with taking
down the Christmas decorations. Like that
bit in Macbeth about how nothing evil goes
about during Christmas-time. The room
looks so bare now, like reality's come back
again. Reality! Sometimes dreams seem more
real than reality. A good dream can make
you feel good all day, and a bad dream can
give you a horrible feeling that gets into
everything you think and do. School starts
again tomorrow, I ought to go to bed, but – I

don't know, I just can't stand the sight of the
bed. I just thought of it just now like a boat
or something and you get strapped into it
when the blankets are on top of you and it
floats you off to places you can't choose –
and just now it's places where I don't want
to go.

It wasn't Billy I dreamed about last night.
That's why I said, isn't it typical. Just when I
was getting this really good relationship
going with Dad, I go and dream about him
and – oh, God, I couldn't even look at him
today without this horrible feeling creeping
over me.

I was in the house alone with him. Not in
the same room though. It wasn't dark outside, not properly. It was a sort of brown
light, sort of creepy, like those old brown-
tinted photos. I knew he'd been drinking
whisky and I suddenly got it into my head
that sometimes people who've been drinking
whisky don't know what they're doing. Then
I thought, the house is awful quiet. And as
soon as I thought that, I could hear this slow,
ticking clock, a big, slow tick, like a grandfather clock, just as if it was trying to make
the house seem quieter. And I thought – he's
dead! He's just sitting down there, with his
whisky glass in his hand and his pipe
between his teeth, being *dead*. All those
thoughts sort of came at once, and somehow

the two ideas got mixed up so that I thought he was dead, but also that he was so drunk he didn't know what he was doing. And then the whole house seemed to be much bigger – huge, room after room, all empty – and I was feeling my way in this horrible brown light down great long corridors and passages and I was sure *he* was following me. And I woke up screaming, Mum, Mum! Tell Dad to stop, tell him to wake up! Only it can't have been out loud, because no one heard me, I just woke up with this awful jolt and lay there sweating – oh, it was horrible. I kept on screaming, Tell him to wake up, over and over: it was strange, I could hear my voice echoing on in my head when I woke up.

I'm going to bed now and I'm going to read one of the Famous Five books. I don't care if it's childish.

What am I going to do about Bucksburn now? I can't trust Dad any more, I just can't. It's so stupid, I feel I'm letting myself be ruled by a dream, but I can't help the way I feel.

January 8th, 1974

OK, Bucksburn. This is the situation.

I must have misjudged him about why he didn't want to go to Blackhall. I might have

known he wasn't interested in dancing at all.
He had other reasons for wanting to go to
Bucksburn, and I still don't know exactly
what they are. I still don't really, really know
if he knows...

It was at the Christmas party at school.
Some of the fifth-year boys had been drinking beer and had got drunk. Tommy
McGeoch was sick on the floor, and one of
the Gordon twins started a fight. I got
pushed and slipped in the yuck. Typical! So I
got my tights cleaned up in the toilet and
then I went out for a bit. It was really cold
and the stars were shining. No, "shining" is a
soft word – they were actually hard and
sparkling, like diamonds. Billy came out to
see if I was all right. I'd been dancing with
him just before that. He's actually quite a
good dancer, compared with some. I said I
was looking at the stars, aren't they lovely,
or something. I was feeling really romantic, it
must have been something to do with the
smell of sick on my tights. We sat on that
little low wall beside the steps, I sat up really
close to him, but he never did anything, he
never reached out at all. I don't know if he
knows what to do. He's never had a girlfriend at all, I think he's really tied up.
Anyway we sat there, and eventually I put
my hand on his shoulder, I thought, I don't
care if he thinks I'm forward. He was all

quiet and I said, What are you thinking about? I always say that to him if he's saying nothing, and he always says, Nothing. I get annoyed at myself for saying it sometimes, but I still go on saying it every time, and he always says, Nothing. So he said, Nothing. Oh well, at least he's predictable.

Then suddenly he said, See how Ally Gordon was carrying on? I'd kill him. He thinks he can act big just because he drinks beer, I hate folk like that. Well, I think the same as him I suppose, but it was the way he said it: I felt really frightened when he said "hate" and "kill". He sounded as if he really hated him enough to actually kill him. I said I'm sure Ally Gordon just behaves like that because he feels inadequate. He said, That's just a big word, it doesn't mean a thing. I love the way he suddenly comes out with things like that. I felt a bit annoyed though too, because I thought he was trying to make me feel small, but then I suddenly got one of those flashes of inspiration and I said, Is amnesia just a big word too? And he just turned and looked at me in that way of his that seems to see right through you. It makes me go all shuddery. And I felt embarrassed and I sort of smiled and said, What? or something like that, and he shook his head and turned away and said OK.

Then there was a long silence and I got up

and said I was going in. I was really cold by
then anyway. But he took hold of me and
pulled me down again. Yes, Billy Stuart actually touched me! Grabbed my wrist and
hauled me back, very romantic, I'm sure. I
didn't try to resist him – I thought, Wow,
this is it. But of course it wasn't. He was
quiet for a bit, then he said, It's not so much
that I don't remember – it's more that I can't
speak. Why not? I said. He shook his head,
then said, There's too many different things I
want to say. What about? I said. He didn't
say anything. I said, Who about? And he put
his head in his hands and rubbed his eyes
really hard and eventually I heard him muttering, Dave Simmers, Dave Simmers, almost
in a sob. I put my hand on his shoulder
again. You can tell me if you want to, I said.
He said, I can't – I can't speak: it's like
there's something in the way so I can't speak.
I said, Do you think going to Bucksburn will
get it out of the way? That was another sort
of inspiration. He said, Maybe.

I suddenly wondered why we were sitting
there talking about all this, and I said, Why
do you want me to go anyway? He just
shrugged. Couldn't you go alone? I said. Or
with Geordie? He just said, I want to go with
you. It was such a lovely thing to say, and he
said it so sort of simply, I got this really
warm feeling spreading all over me, it was

great. He said, Are you going to manage to
get? I said, I'm going to get somehow. He
said, Do you have to tell your mum where
you're going? And I said I'd rather tell them
but if it wasn't going to work I'd cook up
something with Jemma. You'll not tell *her*
anything? he said – that stupid bitch just
opens her mouth and lets her tonsils rattle. I
said, really offended, You're not to talk
about my friend Jemma like that – but I
thought it was so funny, she is an awful gab,
and I'd never tell her anything *really* important that I wanted to keep a secret.

Then I put my arm right round his shoulders – in fact I draped myself all over him. I
wonder if he thinks I feel nice? And I kissed
him on the back of the neck (he'd washed his
hair). I bet he didn't know what had hit him.
Well, the Christmas party's only once a year.
Then I jumped up and said I was going back
in. So in we went. I didn't have the last dance
with him though – I had it with Geordie
Gibbon: ha-ha, serves him right, old slow-
coach. Maybe they'll fight over me.

I've just read this over again. It's really
boring – I said, and he said, and I said...

January 11th, 1974

Decided not to ask about Bucksburn. Jemma

and I are making an "arrangement". I'm staying at her house next Friday night.

CHAPTER
3

RELEASE

Monday morning. Billy listened.

"Well, he shouldn't," his mother's voice came up, shrill but resigned. "It's not right for him. You'll be putting stupid ideas into his head."

A muttering, or a grunt, from his father. Billy carefully folded his school trousers and hung them over the back of the chair. That would cool her down a bit.

Her voice again: "It's me that has to write the letter to the teacher, not you. What am I to say this time?"

Billy pulled on his old oil-blackened jeans and jacket, smacked on his flat canvas cap to keep the hair out of his eyes, and ran down the stairs. It was raining. "Boots," his mother said. "Get those things off." Billy always preferred to go light, in his sandshoes. "If he's to go with you," she said to his father, "he's to wear boots." His father grunted. Billy slipped off his sandshoes, and started hauling his boots on. They didn't feel too bad: cold, wet feet were no fun.

The lorry had already been loaded up at the Yard while Billy had been having his breakfast. Now it stood dripping outside the house, empty except for a tarpaulin-covered mound of something on a wooden pallet roped over the back axle. "What is it?" Billy asked.

"The generator," his father answered. Billy had watched the old generator arrive from the Cottage Hospital, well over a year ago now. He had seen it stripped, taken apart, painstakingly put together again: bit by bit, often with month-long pauses as they waited for some piece of old machinery to turn up and give them just the right cog or spring or needle they needed to get going again. The men's ingenuity and patience in such jobs was incredible, but it all took so long that Billy's interest tended to run out. He had forgotten about the old generator. "Sandy Pirie's needing it," his father explained. "He's no electricity up there."

"Who's Sandy Pirie?" Billy asked.

"You'll see. You've seen him before."

Billy frowned. "I thought we were going up to Peter Ward's."

"We'll see what the weather's doing," his father answered.

63

Billy felt crestfallen. He nearly said he would prefer going to school than a cold, wet run in the lorry to see an old generator unloaded. But it was too late for the school bus now anyway.

"We'll see," his father said again. "Peter's road is on the way anyway."

The rough road up to Peter Ward's hut was not the way they normally went. They normally went on foot up a path that started just across from the Yard and wound up among rough grass and whins and heather, a good five miles. In the fine weather Billy would go some of that way when he went to the Moss, a quiet birch-wood on the north face of the moor where he would catch rabbits – but he would never go as far as Peter Ward's if he was just by himself. But you could also approach from the southern side of the hill, where the slopes were gentler. You had to drive round the hill, by road and then the rough track, but then the walk took little more than ten minutes.

Any boy in Davieburn would jump at the chance of being taken up to Peter Ward's if one of the men from the village was going. You wouldn't talk to the half-crazy old butcher yourself, living up there alone like something from the olden days: you would watch the men talking with him, and sit fascinated by the old man's hawk-like face and calm, terrible, steely eyes.

For two or three months of the winter, Peter Ward would return to civilization and live with his wife in their large house near Couston. Every winter he would drive her around in that year's latest Volvo, visiting relatives and old business friends; he would quarrel with various members of his family and get drunk at Hogmanay. And then, as soon as the first mists of springtime came, he would be restless for a week, and then off, back up to the hills. And there he lived, quite alone, in his old wooden hut, with a stove, a bed, a chair and a table, a pile of *Playboy* magazines, an oil lamp and a shotgun and boxes of cartridges all crammed into the one small room with rough wooden slats for walls, hay spread over the rafters for a ceiling and buckled wooden boards for a floor. A spring of water with a pipe leading to a makeshift cistern was just outside the door. He used the water for making his coffee, but never washed. A few people mentioned sometimes that it was a strange thing, but Peter Ward didn't smell. He ate only the wild things – rabbits, hare, deer and moorland fowl – that he shot, cooking them by dropping them into a pan of deep fat that was always on the stove and was never cleaned out. Billy had once looked into that pan, gazed down into its depths as if he were looking into a gipsy's crystal, wondering at the blackened pieces of bone and feather lying at the bottom. Peter Ward had no beard: rumour had it that he shaved himself with his gutting knife.

It was not that Billy or any of his mates particularly envied the life that Peter Ward led: they were wise enough to appreciate their creature comforts. But it was nourishment to the wild side of their natures to know that someone like Peter Ward was *there*, in existence, and very close to home, living in a way that affronted all decent standards. Peter Ward was no tinker: he had simply seen through all the sham of respectability. And so it was a sort of pilgrimage – or like a journey to a prophet's cave – when any of the village boys were able to pay him a visit.

The lorry splashed through gathering puddles. The door on the passenger side never shut properly, and a spray of fine rain blew in through the crack and wet Billy all down one side. He moved as far away from the door as he could, but he had to keep out of the way of the gear-stick when his father moved up or down gear on the twisting road. All sound was lost in the roar of the old engine.

A couple of miles after passing the Yard they turned off onto a small, single-track road that went up and down, winding around each fold of Craigmore Hill. They passed the end of the rough road that would have taken them to within a mile of Peter Ward's. "I don't mind getting wet," Billy shouted above the noise of the engine. His father said nothing and drove on.

Billy stared out moodily as the rain drove down on grey grass, and grey heather, and the road wound downhill and uphill, in and around. At length, slightly below them, between two long, featureless hills, a group of trees came into view. A pale, sandy-coloured track led towards it, and all around it on the floor of the small glen formed by the two hills, there were brown fields newly sown and pastures neatly fenced off. On the lower slopes of one of the hills Billy could make out the pale grey dots of sheep grazing among the heather.

They came to the beginning of the farm track. The rain was washing the clay to a sandy-coloured milk which was running in two rivers down each side of the track, washing over the compacted stones of the bed.

As they came near the farm, the rain eased and the grey murk of clouds lifted off the hilltops. Wild-eyed bullocks stood in the field adjoining the road and stared at the lorry in its plume of mud.

"Is this where Sandy Pirie lives?" said Billy.

"It is," his father answered.

He brought the lorry hard round into the close behind the farmhouse, and in one practised movement creaked on the handbrake, threw open the cab door and vaulted to the ground. Billy followed, stiff with the raw cold all down his left side.

The next hour and a half was taken up with the job of winching the generator from the lorry and manoeuvring it into its new position in one of the sheds of the close. When Sandy Pirie and his two sons and Will Stuart had satisfied themselves that it was in precisely the right position and had stood looking at it for a good half hour, talking about it and various similar bits of machinery they had had experience of at various times in their lives, they all crossed the close to the back door and trooped in to have dinner in the kitchen. It was not until after the meal, when they were on their second cup of tea, that Sandy Pirie turned to Billy and asked him if he wanted a dog.

Billy was so taken aback he just stared at the farmer. Was he joking, or was he making conversation – or did he really have a dog, or know of one, that he might actually be offering Billy? Billy looked at his father, then back to Sandy Pirie. It was only then it occurred to him that he had seen Sandy Pirie before: this was the same man he had noticed talking with his father on Saturday night at the Bridge, when he had turned round and they were both looking towards him. The same man, only now his natural self, with tousled hair and working clothes that looked a bit as though they were held together with mud and blood and dung. Was it possible his father had suggested this trip today because...? So much went on below the surface with his father.

He shrugged. "I suppose so," he said. He tried to sound indifferent, but his stomach had turned over and his heart had suddenly begun to pound. Was it possible? Might he actually have a dog of his own...? And what would Geordie Gibbon say then?

Sandy Pirie and his father laughed. Billy felt embarrassed: why not come clean? "I wouldn't mind," he tried – but he couldn't say out loud what he was feeling. He hardly knew himself.

Sandy Pirie picked up his cup of tea and began to talk about the lambing that was just starting, and the price of fleeces. Billy looked down at his feet. A dog? If it was from Sandy Pirie's it would most likely be a collie dog, perhaps even a trained dog. Perhaps black, like Dod Moffat's dog, or black and white, with long feathery hair along its sides. Sandy Pirie and his father went on talking about sheep; through the window, the restless rain was blowing over and over; the hands of the kitchen clock crawled round.

There were thirty-five brown specks on the wall above the kitchen range.

Billy let his eyes flicker this way and that, but whatever he tried to look at, whatever he

tried to think of, it always came back to the
one thought: a dog, a dog, a real living dog –
a dog of his own, solid in his hands!

The time ticked on. Billy noticed none of the
amused glances Sandy Pirie was throwing him
over the rim of his tea-cup. He only gradually
became aware that the farmer was speaking of
something else now…

"He was leaping about in front of the tractor," Pirie was saying, "and I never thought
nothing of it. Well, there was a bump, like, but
when I looked back I could see nothing I'd
gone over that would've made a bump like
that. Well, I thought that was queer-kind, but
the dog, well, you wouldn't have thought there
was a thing wrong with him. It wasn't till the
next day that I noticed his back was real stiff
– he was just not willing to get up at all. I got
kind of worried then, so I called the vet, and
blow me if he doesn't say the dog's back's
broken. So it must have been the tractor wheel
that had run over the top of him, and he'd been
running about for the rest of the day with a
broken back! So that was that. We thought
he'd be paralyzed after that, and he was to be
put down, but, well, we left him a bit. He lay
about, oh, for a month fully, and then one day
there he was wandering about the shed, and he
hasn't looked back since."

"But you're not keeping him?" Billy's father
asked.

"No," Sandy Pirie said, "he's gotten out of the way of working. Well, it's near on six months now. It's a long time for a young dog. Och, and he's kind of wasted about the back legs – he can't really walk right. No, I'd decided to shoot him after all."

Billy half suspected that this conversation was a repetition, for his benefit, of a conversation the men had already had – perhaps that night in the Bridge. But it had hooked him: he could contain himself no longer. "You can't shoot him!" he burst out. "Not after all that! He must be a real good dog!"

Sandy Pirie roared with laughter. "Right enough, my lad: he'll be good enough for you – if you want him."

"Is he here?" Billy said. "What's his name?"

"Come and see him," Pirie said. He got up, put on his cap and jacket, and went out to the door. Billy and his father followed.

On the ground outside the back door there was a pile of old plastic baler-twine, a bright tangle of orange and pale blue and yellow. Sandy Pirie bent and eased out a length of the orange. He handed it to Billy: "You'll need that." They crossed the close, and Pirie went to a lean-to shed with a green door that had a couple of brown boards nailed across the bottom where the original boards must have rotted. The door was tied shut. Pirie fiddled about with the wet knot for a moment before

71

taking out his pocket knife and cutting through the string. He pushed the door open and stood back for Billy.

It was very dark in the shed, and the smell of dog dirt almost overpowering. Billy could see nothing at first. Then his eyes began to make out a couple of splashes of white at the far end, on the floor. He went nearer. It was only after staring for a minute that he began to make them out. He was looking at a dog half on its back. Its belly was white, and the fore-leg that was held up straight – in a gesture, almost, of helpless pleading – was also white, as if it had a sock on. White about the shoulder, a white tail-tip, and a pale muzzle that was not quite white. The eyes were rolled forward because of the dog's position half on its back: they were watching Billy intently, showing dim crescents of white at their upper rims. They looked purple in that light. The dog was quite motionless, in his ridiculous posture, the back legs splayed out, the feathery tail curled tightly up between them. But there was a ten-sion and alertness about him as well. His lips were curled up a little, partially baring his teeth, but the expression was unmistakably a smile.

Billy squatted down. The dog remained motionless, but his nose puckered a little, its black button wiggling to and fro. He was taking stock.

72

"Drift. Drift. Here." Sandy Pirie's voice came from behind Billy. The white tip of the dog's tail moved a little, wagging almost apologetically next to his belly, and then went still. He made no other movement.

"You come out first, Billy," his father said. "Give him room."

Billy felt already half in a dream. He got up, and backed slowly out of the shed. "You call him," Sandy Pirie said. "See what he does."

"Drift," Billy said; but his voice was a hoarse whisper. "Drift," he tried again, louder. "Come, Drift."

And suddenly the dog moved. For an instant his legs waved stupidly in the air; then he rolled over onto them, bounded out of the shed, and was weaving excitedly about their feet, as Billy and his father turned this way and that trying to get a proper look at him.

He was not black. He was a ruddy colour, only a shade darker than a fox, like a mixture of coffee and blood. He had a broad, dashing feathery white ruff at his collar, a pink nose, and strange chocolatey-golden eyes. He was powerfully built at the shoulders, but from halfway down his back he narrowed abruptly, and his hindquarters might have belonged to a different dog, they were so much more slender. His back legs looked as if he didn't quite have them under control, though he ran fluently enough. There was something about him

73

which reminded Billy of an articulated lorry, as if you could simply unhitch the hindquarters from the forequarters and let him run on two legs.

For a moment Billy's mind rejected the dog: it was not exactly deformed, but there was something verging on deformity. But in that same moment Drift turned and his strange golden eyes looked straight into Billy's, and instantly he knew that the two of them could not now go their separate ways. There was no question: Drift would go home with Billy.

"Put the string round his neck and take him a wee walk," Sandy Pirie said. "Don't take him off though, for there's sheep about."

So Billy took Drift for a walk along the stony road they had come down on the lorry, with the milky water flowing over the surface, Drift walking along beside Billy, neither jerking forward nor putting his heels in but occasionally turning to look sidelong at him, as if making sure his pace was matched to Billy's. Billy looked down at the thin orange line that joined the dog's neck to his own hand. It seemed like a lifeline, joining his own thoughts and wishes to Drift's, but as a lead it was quite unnecessary. Whenever they came in sight of sheep, Drift would drop down onto his belly, his chin flat along the ground, his eyes, seeming to grow paler, staring wickedly; but when Billy said nothing his eyes would waver, and then roll back under puckering brows to glance up at him in a short, unanswered appeal. Then he would get up again, as if he had heard Billy's thought – you can't go after sheep now, Drift, you've got to forget about sheep. And then he would rise and walk on, as before, carefully matching his pace to Billy's.

They left not long after Billy and Drift returned to the farmhouse. Drift was almost as much trouble to get onto the lorry as the generator had been to get off. He had been run over once by a tractor: now, it seemed, he was frightened of any vehicle with a loud engine. Even when Billy's father turned the engine off and Billy climbed into the cab and called him, Drift cowered and would not go near. In the end Sandy Pirie picked him up by the scruff of the neck and the tail and flung him unceremoniously in, while Billy slammed the door shut. He felt like a traitor to the dog he wanted only trust from, but Drift seemed unperturbed by the treatment: he sat on the floor with his chin pressed flat across Billy's knees, looking intently up into his eyes.

"One thing you'll need to watch," Sandy Pirie shouted in through the window: "don't let him go after sheep. If he does, you'll have to give him a good thrashing. It's kindest in the long run. He's used to it, mind: he's worked sheep ever since he was a pup." The noise of the engine drowned out the rest of his words.

"I'm never going to hit him," Billy said passionately as they turned out of the close onto the farm road.

"It's better than having him shot," his father replied.

"How, shot?" Billy said, taken aback.

"If he's caught going after sheep," his father answered, "he'll get shot, and you can't blame any farmer for doing it."

"No one's going to shoot Drift," Billy said. "Whatever happens."

Package 5

Hobart
June 16, 1984

Dear Roger,

You'll probably notice (if males ever
notice such things) that what the entry
of January 19th (enclosed) *fails* to
mention is the name of the young fellow
Jemma was out with while I was busy
with my evening of - well, you'll read
about it. I don't put much trust in the
male memory when it comes to such triv-
ial details so there's no point in
saying "correct me if I'm wrong"… But
it was your first night out with her,
wasn't it? And I bet you never knew she
was in such an emotional state the next
day, either - but of course that was
nothing to do with you…

T.T.

DIARY

January 15th, 1974

I forgot to mention when I was writing about
the Christmas party: Geordie Gibbon's leaving the area. I felt really strange when I first
heard about it. I still don't know quite what
to think now, either. Geordie was the first
boy I had any real – well, feelings for. And he
really had a rough time last term, over his
dad and all that. He hasn't come back this
term at all. I think his mother's got a job at
some school down in Ayrshire. Geordie says
it's all going to be new and strange: maybe
that's for the best anyway. He rang me up
yesterday to tell me they were going at the
weekend. He asked me if I'd like to go over
and see him on Friday evening. That's the
night I'll be staying with Jemma, but it's also
the night I was supposed to be going to
Bucksburn with Billy. I don't know why but I
put Billy off. I think he was offended, but I
told him I'd go with him later, perhaps in a
fortnight. I'll get Jemma to come over and
stay here next weekend, so that Mum thinks
it's just some new ritual we've started, week
and week about. I didn't tell Billy why I
wasn't going – I made some excuse about
putting Jemma's mum off her guard. I don't

know what he'd think about it. He and
Geordie have never been close again since the
Accident and everything, even though they
did make up after they'd stopped talking for
so long.

Geordie phoned me up to tell me what
was happening – about Ayrshire and all that.
Mum doesn't mind Geordie as much as Billy,
even now. I suppose that's because he's
Middle Class, however much mess his dad
goes and gets into. I had to ring off quicker
than I meant to though, because as he was
telling me about going away I began to get
this awful lump in my throat, and I couldn't
even talk properly and I knew I was going to
start crying. Emotions are funny things. I
keep on wanting to cry nowadays, at all sorts
of silly things. Mrs Mayer was talking about
amoebas in biology today and how they split
into two, and even that made me want to
cry! God, what a state, getting upset over the
Lowest Form of Life.

Anyway, I'm looking forward to Friday. I
have to admit I'm looking forward to it more
now than when I'd been going to go to
Bucksburn. I must be going through a reac-
tion to Billy. I wonder if it'll last. When I was
first friendly with Geordie, he and Billy were
best friends. I never got to know Billy at all
at that time though. Geordie seemed to have
two separate lives going on, one when he was

friends with Billy, and one when he was
being more – well, this is what I thought –
more himself. I only saw Billy sort of at a distance at that time, and I couldn't really see
what Geordie had in common with him. Not
that I ever asked Geordie about him, and he
hardly mentioned Billy at all. It's really
funny, when I think about it, because I used
to talk about Jemma all the time.

Billy always looked sort of – I don't know
– a bit sort of rough, I suppose. His hair was
long too, and sometimes he wore sandshoes
to school and got into trouble. He never
spoke back to them though – he never gave
them cheek. Even Geordie would sometimes
give them cheek, but Billy was just – sullen.
Actually it was only once a week that we
were even in the same class, so I don't really
know.

I know I thought he must be a bit stupid.
Now that I've started to think more about
things like that, I know it was all just Class
Prejudice. I was seeing Billy through my
mother's eyes. I've never spoken to Billy
about when I was friendly with Geordie. I
realize now that Billy thought Geordie was
really soft – so I suppose Billy must have
changed too. Maybe it was Drift that
changed him. Anyway, he *is* different, and
Geordie wouldn't have told Billy about me
then, because Billy would have laughed at

him if he'd thought he had a girlfriend. Well, maybe it's going a bit far to say I was his girlfriend exactly. It was over a year ago. Looking back, I feel I must have been totally stupid and handless then. I mean, we kissed and things like that, but... Well there wasn't so much *of* me then. I mean...

I don't know if I should write down the bit I was just going to write, in case someone reads it.

No, that's stupid: it's my diary, and I can write what I like in it. And if Mum reads it and gets shocked, then it's her own fault and she shouldn't have been reading it in the first place. She's got no right. At the Christmas party, one of the fifth-year boys asked me to have a dance with him. He wasn't one of the drunk ones: I don't know what his name is, but I know he's in the football team. He's sort of big and – muscly, I suppose. He's quite nice. At least, to look at: I'm not sure if he's nice in character or not. As we were dancing, I couldn't help noticing he kept looking at my – well, my chest; and after the music stopped he just remarked, quite casually, You've got nice tits; and then went away. I still can't really sort out what I thought. I mean, it was a pretty disgusting thing to say, really. I suppose. I mean, he might have meant it as a compliment – or I suppose he might even have meant it as an

>

insult: what about the rest of me? What about *me*? I heard this woman in a play on the TV – she was saying to her husband, I just feel like an object, or something. That's just how it made me feel. At least – a bit of me felt like that: maybe that other, completely adult bit of me. But the other bit of me – it's awful really, and I suppose it's all wrong – the other bit of me was so elated, I thought, wow, he's seventeen and he looks pretty grown-up really – and I turn him on! I went and told Jemma and she said some terrible things – she really does have a mind like a drain.

Yet for all that, it's so difficult working out what you really feel like. I mean, I said it was the grown-up part of me that felt disgusted by what he said. But maybe I'm just assuming it's the grown-up part of me that thinks that way, because of what the woman said on TV – she must have been thirty at least. But it's strange that I should feel all silly and young when it's an older boy that likes me (supposing he meant that he did like me), and yet it's with a younger boy that the more grown-up part of me comes out – I mean, with Billy. Or Geordie. Geordie and I just kissed, he never put his hands anywhere he wasn't supposed to. Once he held me round the waist, but that's as *low* as he got. But my *feelings* with Geordie were really seri-

ous: they were deep feelings, or at least I felt
they were at the time. But what that boy said
to me had the opposite effect: it made me go
silly and giggly – and I was excited, I have to
admit it. I feel really deeply involved with
Billy, and that day last year when I finished
things with Geordie, even though it was me
that finished it, I cried all evening the day I
did it. I can't even remember why it was
now. Thinking about Geordie now, I know
that, deep down, I'm still really fond of him.
Or do I mean I love him? Do I mean I love
Billy as well? Love's such a little word, but
it's such a big thing – I get frightened even to
see myself writing it down on paper.

January 19th, 1974

Now what am I to think. Geordie and I sat in
his room and talked for about an hour. They
don't actually do their flitting till Sunday, so
the furniture was still there, and he'd left his
posters up on the wall, he said it was for me
so that it would look more homely. Then his
mother came in and said she was just going
out to see a neighbour and would we be all
right. Well, we *were* all right! What an amazing difference from a year ago! Nothing like
that's ever happened to me before. We were
on the bed and – kissing, and – kissing and…

We were all over each other. I mean we got *really* close. It was a lovely experience. I put my hands inside his shirt (I undid it first); and I let him do the same to me. I had on my blouse with the lacy collar. When I read this over in a couple of days' time I'm going to be really embarrassed. I don't think it's the sort of thing you can write about properly anyway.

Oh God, and now he's going away. I don't know what to do with myself. I've got this burning feeling in the pit of my stomach. No, I'm not going to think about that, or I'll get the way I was all morning. I'm just going to think about the positive side of it, how good it felt. I felt really good when I got back to Jemma's afterwards, but next morning when I woke up, I felt – oh, I don't know what I felt. I felt sad, sad, like a huge ocean of sadness inside me: I could almost see it inside me, all silvery grey, seagulls gliding over it making little whining noises. And I knew this was going to have to rise up, it was just going to have to rise and pour out of me some time.

I felt sad about everything, just everything. About Billy and everything he'd gone through, and about Drift, and about what I'd done to him – I mean, I don't exactly feel guilty because, well, Billy's never really even touched me, properly, and it's as if he doesn't

really like me *that* way; but somehow I felt
he wouldn't really like it if he knew that
Geordie and I had got together like that –
and I felt sorry for him. And I felt so, so sad
about Geordie going as well, and about
everything that he's been through, and it's
just not fair. Jemma was feeling really happy
because of this new boyfriend she's got – he's
in sixth year – and she was trying to be really
cheery and talk about all sorts of other
things, but after breakfast I just couldn't hold
it back any longer, and I sat in her room and
howled and howled. I must have howled for
two hours solid. I don't think she knew what
to do with me. Anyway in the end she joined
in and we sat and howled together. I feel a
bit better now. I sat in Jemma's room all
afternoon with cold, wet cloths over my eyes
so that Mum wouldn't see I'd been crying
when I got home. Jemma's mum looked at
me and said, Oh, boyfriend trouble, I suppose, and I nodded and wanted to laugh and
cry at the same time.

January 24th, 1974

I haven't spoken to Billy all week. Not properly, I mean. I couldn't bring myself to on
Monday and Tuesday, and on Wednesday
and today I was off school with a cold. It's

not really a bad cold, but I made Mum think it was worse than it actually is. I'll have to go back tomorrow though, or she won't let Jemma come to stay here in the evening.

CHAPTER
4

PREY

Round Davieburn itself there were no good places for going out with a dog. There was the old railway track, certainly, but it was bordered by farms all along its length, and Billy soon found that Drift could clear a fence in a single leap. He would run straight towards it, and seemed only at the very last moment to decide whether it was a fence he could go through or one he would have to go over. Having decided, he would seem to fling himself up into the air rather than merely jump, all four legs together, and for a split second you would see him hanging above the fence, like an aeroplane with its undercarriage lowered; then he would be down on the other side and running as if he had never been interrupted. The amount of ground he covered in a single sprint astonished and alarmed Billy, and he decided he would have to take him somewhere where there were no sheep or cattle or horses, at least until they got to know each other better.

The quickest and easiest way to get away from the farm country was to get a lift up to the Yard with his father. The spring was coming on, the days were lengthening, and his father would go up to the Yard after their evening meal if there was some work he wanted to finish. Then Billy would take Drift over the road and up onto the lower slopes of Craigmore Hill, where he could walk or run with him for miles, as the dusk deepened in the valley-land behind them. On this side of the hill, and over as far as Peter Ward's hut, was wild land, with heather, rough grass and broom, and here and there small woods of birch and pine.

One of these woods was the Moss, where Billy had used to go to catch rabbits. Up there, among the ferns and the long grass under the birch trees in summertime, or among the deep heather at the edge of the wood where all the rabbit-holes were, he had used to lie, two hours at a stretch, waiting for the rabbits to get used to his smell in the air, letting them become careless to the danger. He would lie still and quiet as a log all that time, on his belly, his elbows out to the sides, his hands gripping the ground in front of him, breathing lightly and quite soundlessly through his nose. If he chose the right spot, sooner or later a rabbit would always come within reach; always it would stop, alert, ready to bolt, sensing it was nearer the intruder than it had been. Billy would not move, although now his whole body would be tense, ready. The rabbit's alertness would give way to uncertainty: it would rub its face with its forepaws, or bite its haunch. Still Billy would wait. Not until it had bent its head, nosed the grass, nibbled, would he move: then he would pounce, projecting himself forward with elbows, knees and toes. It would have been a hard way to hunt if he had been really hungry: he had not caught more than half a dozen rabbits that way, though he had never given up trying. The first he had caught he had killed – a sharp blow to the back of its head with a stick, and the whole family had enjoyed rabbit stew. He had never been able to do that again, though he had often intended to: he had held his prey instead, cradled in his arms, stroking the long ears flattened down on its back, feeling the shaking of its heart, warily watching the explosive bead-like eyes, ready to pre-empt any bid to escape, delighting in his skill as a hunter, but unable to finish the hunter's task.

Perhaps it was the influence of Geordie Gibbon. Billy often despised Geordie for being a bit soft. But he also had a grudging respect for him – not that he would ever have admitted it. A certain gentleness and delicacy about

Geordie – less in what he said than in the way he acted, in his movements and gestures, in the fact that he was able to talk sensibly with girls – had probably had more influence on Billy than he realized.

But everything was changed now.

When Billy first went up the Moss one Sunday with Drift, he lay down in the heather, got Drift to lie beside him, and put one hand gently on the dog's neck. It was hopeless.

Billy had thought, having seen Drift lying and staring out the sheep, that he would have a lot of patience. He had thought of the understanding between them, and believed Drift would take his cue and lie still and silent too. But Drift twitched and fidgeted, raised his nose to sniff the air, kicked Billy with those back legs of his which never seemed completely under control, or turned to lick him in the ear or bury his nose snuffling among his hair. Billy got furious, Drift became offended – he sulked, mooching off, pointedly lifting his leg against trees and tussocks, as if to say: I'm a dog, and I've got my way of doing things.

And, naturally, he had. He could catch rabbits far better than Billy ever could, hurtling down on them with all his weight and force, breaking their backs with his jaws and killing them almost on the instant he touched them.

Billy himself gave up hunting, and let Drift have his own way. If he decided to take the dead rabbit for the family, Drift would let him without a murmur. If he decided to let him keep it, Drift would crunch up his prey as he ran, swallowing it whole, skin, fur and all, within thirty seconds. Then, when they stopped, he would bring it all back up again, and slaver and crunch at leisure like a gourmet. Billy would watch, repelled and fascinated. He had never seen a dog behave like this. Rob's greyhound was as delicate in her eating habits as one of the fur-coated patrons of the Bridge Restaurant: taking a mouthful or two from her dish, then trotting off, lifting her head to look round in every direction before elegantly returning for a little more. Sometimes Billy regretted no longer being able to hold the rabbits he caught, to stroke their fur and then let them go. Sometimes the strangeness of Drift's presence forced itself in on him. Feeling close to the dog as he did, often he found himself expecting it to have human thoughts and reactions. To see Drift slavering on a piece of sodden rabbit skin, his muzzle dark with blood, he was struck sharply with a sense of having taken something alien and wild into his life.

One evening Billy was coming down off the rough hill with Drift when he saw below a high-sided white van toiling up towards the Yard. It was dusk, and the van glimmered;

only its sidelights were on, twinkling between fence posts and sparsely leaved bushes. Billy guessed at once it was Dave Simmers. He went on down the path until, just coming out of the last thick belt of whin-bushes, he saw his father and Andy Gibbon at the gate of the Yard. His father's van and Andy Gibbon's BMW were sitting there, and both men were leaning against the car, his father with his arm stretched across its roof. In the failing light the car looked the colour of clotted blood. Billy stopped, watching. The two men looked as though they were waiting for someone. If it had been just his father, Billy would have thought it was himself he was waiting for. But not Andy Gibbon as well.

Will Stuart looked relaxed, leaning against the BMW, almost caressing its roof with the one hand, gesticulating in his energetic way with the other as he talked. But there was something tense and alert about Andy Gibbon as he faced him. Then Dave Simmers' van swept round the corner and stopped.

Will Stuart half turned, his arm still on the roof of the car, and then rolled round so that he was leaning with his back against it. Andy Gibbon had straightened up from the car, and was standing now with his thumbs in his belt. Dave Simmers turned off the engine of his van. For a moment Billy heard a curlew calling, then the high, curdling whoop was switched off and the whole scene became dead still.

Billy glanced down at Drift, and stiffened. Drift's way, if Billy ever stopped to look around, was to sit beside him, his shoulders hunched, his ears hanging limply over to the sides, and peer around at nothing in particular. But when Billy looked down now, Drift was flattened along the ground, glaring down towards the three men at the gate of the Yard, looking for all the world as if he had come face to face with a strong-minded ewe that intended going on without the flock. He was dead silent, and the hair down his back was slightly raised, menacing.

Billy frowned. Drift's behaviour puzzled him, and yet in some dim way he understood it as well. There was nothing particularly remarkable about Dave Simmers appearing up at the Yard, but it was a strange time of the day to make an appointment for: and Billy felt sure that, for Andy Gibbon at least, this was an appointment. Andy Gibbon looked very ill at ease.

Billy looked at his father again. He was still leaning with his back to the car, both hands now grasping the straps of his dungarees. For all that he seemed relaxed, something about him suggested that the relaxation was forced: with his hands hanging onto the dungaree straps at his chest, he almost looked as if he were about to start boxing. Billy knew his father's movements and gestures well: more than many boys, he had spent a lot of time with his father, especially when he was younger and had hung about the Yard most of the time. There was something about the way his father had turned round when Dave Simmers appeared which Billy found infinitely disturbing...

Dave Simmers and Andy Gibbon moved away further into the Yard.

That was it! It was the way you looked if the teacher came in, and you didn't know if he'd noticed you doing whatever it was you weren't supposed to. And his father had looked that way at Dave Simmers – his father, who was at least twice Dave Simmers' age. Older men simply didn't react to younger men that way.

At that moment his father looked up and saw Billy, and called to him. Billy came down slowly, Drift, who hardly ever needed a leash now, walking close in at his heel. In a way, Billy was relieved to have been seen and called. In the scene he had just witnessed, there was something which threatened to turn the world's scale of values upside down, and his mind turned eagerly to something that would divert it.

They drove home in silence, leaving Andy Gibbon to put the padlock on the gate.

* * *

The following Saturday, Billy went over to
Geordie's house with Drift. He didn't often go
over there: normally Geordie would knock
him up at his house, or they would more often
have agreed to wait at the gate of the old railway track and would go off out of the village
from there. Billy felt ill at ease in Geordie's
house. It was a substantial old manse-house on
the outskirts of the village and it had roses
trailing up round the front door. Geordie's
mother was a teacher, not at their own school
but at one of the primary schools, and she was
very strict about muddy shoes. Geordie's sister
had a pony, and they kept twelve black hens
in a neatly fenced run at the end of the vegetable garden.

Mrs Gibbon looked askance at the panting
collie standing on the doorstep with Billy,
peering past her legs as if about to invite itself
in.

"Is he house-trained?" she said.

"I don't know," Billy stumbled. "He's never
done it in the house, but I've to keep him in the
shed with Rob's dog at night."

"George!" Mrs Gibbon called. "You'd
better stay outside with him, Billy. George'll
be down in a minute." She shut the door. Drift
looked mournfully up at Billy.

"It's no matter, Drift," Billy said. "We like
it better outside anyway." He looked over the
back garden. There was a washing-green,

95

some apple-trees, then the vegetable garden beyond that with the hen-run at the end. Someone had left the run gate open, and the black hens were all over the vegetable patch, pecking and scratching in the newly raked soil. Drift was watching them intently.

"Drift," Billy whispered, scarcely audible. "Sh – away by, Drift!"

When Geordie came out, Billy was standing in the washing-green, not quite knowing whether to be looking innocently in the opposite direction, away over the garden wall towards the hills, or whether to be watching proudly the goings-on in the vegetable garden. Either way, there Drift was, trotting backwards and forwards; and there the hens were, gathered together in a bunch, being driven inexorably towards the gate of their run.

Geordie gaped. "Did you tell him to do that?"

Billy parried. "He can do that kind of thing. He's been trained to it."

"What, with hens?"

"No, with sheep. But it's the same thing. Were they supposed to be out?" Billy was a little anxious, in case he was caught interfering.

"I don't know," Geordie said. "Can I see him doing it again?"

Billy called Drift back. "Give them a few minutes," he said.

"OK, five," Geordie said. They waited five

minutes – Geordie's eyes glued to his watch as he counted out the seconds – till the hens had scattered over the garden again. Then again Billy gave the command: "Away by!" – this time in a clear, commanding voice.

And this time, it was the real thing: Drift streaked off round the garden perimeter, his red and white coat, whenever he slowed and turned, making almost a splash of colour among the duns and greys of the garden. Round the hens he went, then round again, gathering them into a loose, then into a tighter, knot; then he flung himself down to one side of them, his chin flat along the ground, his eyes gleaming with menace. Irresolutely, the hens began to move towards the gate again.

"That's great!" said Geordie, genuinely impressed. "Can I make him do it?"

Billy felt uncertain about this. "I don't know if he'd do it for you," he said. "He's used to me."

"I'll try," Geordie said. "Drift!" he called. "Here, Drift."

And Drift came.

"Sit," said Geordie.

Drift lay down.

This time, Geordie was not going to wait for the hens to scatter. He ran among them, chasing them here and there, while Billy squatted beside Drift with a restraining hand on his neck.

"You'll not do it for him, Boy, will you?" he said. Drift looked back up at him, his tongue lolling, his golden eyes rolling.

The kitchen window opened. "What do you think you're doing, George?"

"Look, Mum," Geordie called back. "Look what you can make Drift do." He came back and stood beside Billy. "Now, Drift," he said breathlessly: "sh – away by!"

Billy bit his lip. Drift went. His blood was up, the praise had got into him. He went at it a little too excitedly, and one of the hens flew squawking into an apple-tree. Then he checked himself, gave them room, and the hen flew down and scuttled back to join the flock. This time he put them right into the hen-run and then lay in the entrance, his nose working with the unfamiliar smell.

Geordie's mother watched for a minute, then shut the window and turned away.

"That's what a bairn does," Billy said scornfully. "Shouts for his mam to come and see what he can do."

"What do you mean?" Geordie said, surprised. "She was just going to tell us to leave the hens alone. That's why I got her to watch. Drift?" he called. "Come here, Drift."

Drift came back to them. Geordie knelt down and touched noses with him and fondled his ears.

"You're not to do that." Billy was almost

surprised at the sound of his own voice.

"Not to do what?" Geordie said.

"You're not to pet him," Billy answered firmly. "It'll spoil him."

"Who says?"

"Everyone does. You're not supposed to pet a working dog."

"But he's a pet," Geordie said. "He's not a working dog."

"Look, I've said how I want him treated – right?" Billy was flushed with anger.

"I don't see what's wrong with clapping him."

"If you don't do what I say," Billy shouted, "you're not going to get to come for a walk with him."

Geordie stepped back a pace. Billy had never seen him look so surprised and hurt. He knew that he was being unreasonable, that pure jealousy was making him act childishly himself; but he couldn't draw back.

"All right," Geordie said at last. "All right, you go on and have a walk with him. You know the way out." He turned and stalked back into the house, closing the door quietly behind him. Drift followed him a few paces and then returned to Billy's heel, whining softly.

"Come, Drift." Billy crossed the grass to the gate. His hand was trembling as he shut it behind him and he couldn't replace the catch properly.

It was the last time he and Geordie were to speak to each other for two months.

Billy walked blindly for quarter of an hour, Drift never leaving his heel. "It was his fault," he muttered once, picking up a stone and flinging it savagely into a mass of frog spawn in the ditch by the roadside. The jelly broke apart, and jelly and water mixed spurted onto the side of the bank. Drift went down to sniff at it, then returned to Billy's heel.

Billy looked round to take stock of where he was. He decided to take a short cut home, across the fields: Duncan's farm, Simmers' farm, Wilson's farm, and back. He jumped the ditch, squeezed between two plain wires of the fence on the far side, and started off in a straight line towards the two old sheds in the second of Simmers' fields. The only livestock they passed was two cows with calves at the far end of one of Sandy Duncan's fields, but they showed no interest in Drift and Drift showed none in them.

The two old sheds in Luncarty land, the Simmers' farm, were part of an old farm steading long out of use. There had been other buildings as well, but they were ruins now. Here and there, a part of a gable end jutted up, but for the most part all you could see of the old farm was the ground plan of its buildings mounded in the green grass. The two standing sheds were dilapidated, their roofs bellied in. An ancient, rusty harrow lay there, and a roller that was free of rust, obviously still in use. A heap of wood and rusty corrugated tin lay up against one of the walls. Everywhere beside the stones and the grass-covered ruins reddish spikes of nettles were pushing up.

As they passed the first shed, a small brown shape ran out just in front of Billy's feet. Drift was after it in a flash, but it dodged under a large stone. Billy ran to the stone and pushed it up slightly, and Drift thrust his nose in, snuffling and snorting. The stone was heavy; Billy managed to push it up a little more, Drift thrust his head in a little farther, and – "Go on, Drift, quick!" – the brown thing darted out from the other side of the stone and made for the second shed. It was a rat.

Drift whipped his head out, shaking it and sneezing earth out of his nose, and then gave chase. He headed the rat off from the door of the shed, but it darted round the side. Drift lost a second as the momentum of his ill-controlled back legs carried his hindquarters slithering forward even as his forelegs were changing direction. Then both rat and dog disappeared round the side of the shed.

When Billy caught up, Drift was snuffling and digging furiously beside the heap of long pieces of timber and tin against the wall. Billy bent down to look, and lifted one of the sheets

101

of tin. One of the sticks of timber rolled off it, clattering loudly. Billy threw off the sticks. Drift was in a frenzy, and the dog's urgency was infecting the boy. He pulled away more timber from the bottom of the pile, and lifted more of the sheets of tin to try and let Drift in. For a moment he thought he actually saw the rat's eye gleaming, but it disappeared again. It seemed strange it hadn't gone further inside the pile.

Drift dived into the space Billy was opening up. For a moment he was digging madly, then something clanked – a harsh, metallic noise – and the whole pile shifted slightly. Drift gave a small yelp of fright, backed out, and then ran round to the other end of the pile.

Billy peered under the corrugated sheets he was holding up. He couldn't see anything clearly at first, but straining into the gloom he began to make out long, regular rows of something that gleamed dully. He frowned, knelt down, and still holding up the tin with one hand, stretched the other hand in underneath. Smooth, cold, cylindrical things that clanked when you moved them. Pipes, it had to be. From the dullness of their gleam, Billy guessed they were copper pipes. At any other time, he would have thought little enough of it, and even now his attention was divided between the pipes and the rat; but something his father had said ran through his head, about the price of copper rocketing because of some kind of shortage.

It was strange. He withdrew his hand, let the tin and timber fall again. It made a loud clank. He stood up and scratched his head, puzzled. He was watching Drift scrabbling at the other end of the pile, but he was preoccupied.

"And just what do you think you're doing?" The voice from behind Billy jolted him like an electric shock, and at the same instant Drift rushed forward, barking furiously.

It was Dave Simmers. It had to be, of course. He always had to be there behind you, watching over your shoulder. Drift stopped a yard away from him, sniffing threateningly, his hackles raised all down his back.

"What are you doing?" Dave Simmers asked again. He was tall, heavy-built, with dark curly hair, a blank pale face that was inclined to show up red marks, and restless, flicking eyes. His fleshy mouth never smiled. At this moment his face carried even less expression than usual, and his eyes flickered over Billy almost as if he were having difficulty seeing him. His face was a mask – whether he was angry or alarmed, amused or curious was impossible to tell. Only three things were certain: his face was never pleasant, he was twice as strong as Billy, and there was no one else

103

around. Drift growled softly. Dave Simmers ignored him.

"Well?" His eyes became still. They were like stones.

"My dog was chasing a rat," Billy said at last. "Did you know you had rats here?"

"What's it got to do with you? What were you doing here in the first place?"

"It's a free country," Billy said. "I'm doing no harm."

"What were you looking at there?"

"Nothing. I was looking for the rat."

"There's no rat there," Dave Simmers said.

"Aye, there is," Billy said stoutly, but his heart was quailing in him. "I saw it running in there."

"I said there's no rat there," Dave Simmers repeated tonelessly.

"Look—" Billy began.

"What did you find?" Dave Simmers was persistent, but at the same time he seemed to be only half there, as if he were thinking of something else. He had working-boots on with steel toecaps, but the green boiler suit he was wearing was almost spotless. His hands were in his pockets, a mockery of a relaxed attitude.

"I told you—" Billy tried to say. His tongue felt dry.

"You're going to get your head kicked in," Dave Simmers said, softly, with emphasis.

"You're going to get your head kicked in if I *ever* find you poking your ugly little nose round here again."

A ray of hope. Perhaps he would get away with it. "All right," Billy said. "I won't come here again." But cold fear was tingling down his back.

Drift had crept closer to Dave Simmers' leg. His hackles were still up. He stretched his nose out and sniffed the bottom of the boiler suit. Without warning, Dave Simmers lashed out sideways with his boot. He missed, and Drift bounded back unharmed, but he was growling openly now and his teeth were bared.

"Set your dog on me, would you!" Dave Simmers erupted.

"I never did!"

Dave Simmers took two sudden steps forward, grabbed at Billy's collar and twisted it up, pulling Billy almost off his feet. Billy cried out with anger, but he felt like jelly: the strength of Dave Simmers' hand was astonishing. "I never!" he shouted. "Drift! Drift, come on!"

And with his teeth bared, with a long spluttering growl that was almost a roar, Drift sprang.

Dave Simmers and Billy staggered a pace as the dog's weight made its impact. Dave Simmers let go of Billy, who fell on one knee. Drift had lost the momentum of his spring, but he

105

was ready to come again. In that split second Dave Simmers shifted his weight and let fly with a savage kick at Drift's head.

The steel toecap caught the dog full on the jaw. Drift yelped, then rolled right over and back onto his feet. For a moment he was silent, holding his head in a queer, pained, twisted way, then suddenly he let out a terrible yelping howl, turned with his tail locked tight between his legs, his back rounded, and galloped off, yelping continuously, through the fence and out of sight.

"Drift!" Billy called desperately. And then Dave Simmers was on him, and he felt himself whirled up off his feet, then an excruciating, jarring crunch as Dave Simmers' boot caught him fairly between the buttocks, then for an instant he was sailing through the air towards the barbed-wire fence. His face and body missed it, but it caught his left leg as he went over, so that his chest crashed down hard onto the ground, winding him, while his trouser leg and his shin were torn all down by the rusty spike. He rolled over, splashing into the ditch on the far side, gasping for air.

"Now get!" He heard Dave Simmers' voice through the roaring in his head; "and keep your bloody mouth shut!"

The breath sobbed back into his lungs. He was his own master again, no longer an object to be sent flying through the air or dropped in a ditch. He scrambled up, aching groin, bleeding leg, torn and sodden clothes and all, and ran.

Package 6

Hobart
June 30, 1984

Dear Roger,

The next chapter of the story contains
an account of the first meeting –
depicted, I may say, with utmost
restraint – between Billy Stuart and
me. I am mentioning it because I expect
you to be equally restrained in your
response. I'm not used to writing about
myself like a character in a story, and
I can tell you it wasn't easy!

   But first you can read the diary.

A.E.

T.T.

DIARY

February 3rd, 1974

I suppose I'd better write about the Great
Excursion, because I'll probably just wish I
had later if I don't. Not that I actually feel
like doing it – I mean, it was all right – eventually. For me, anyway. I'm not sure about
Billy. I suppose I'm just getting a bit fed up
with his whole big quest thing. It's just a way
of getting attention, I think. Well, he's got
my attention – what more does he want?

The plan worked fine, as far as Mum
went. It's quite a good way of getting out
places at the weekend, I don't know why I
didn't think about it before. Too honest, I
suppose. The dutiful daughter. Well, it's
Mum's own fault: she's no right not giving
me my freedom. No one else of fifteen would
put up with a mother like her. The only trouble was I'd taken my dress to wear and I had
to stuff it in the bottom of my bag, so it was
all creased when I took it out, and Jemma
had told her mum we were just going to the
café in Blackhall, so I had the problem of getting it straightened out and *then* the problem
of getting it on without Jemma's mum noticing. Another time I'll take something I can
wear *either* to the café or the disco. Jemma

said we could work on her mum about the Blackhall disco, but we didn't want to mention discos at all this time in case Mum checked up with Jemma's mum at all.

Anyway, that's all irrelevant. Well, it's not, but it's got nothing to do with Billy's Big Thing. That sounds rude. We smuggled the iron into Jemma's room, and pressed my dress on the carpet there – it was the only flat, hard surface she's got. I put on my long coat, and then we waited until the very last moment before we left her room – normally her mum likes to see what we're wearing – but we left it till the last moment and then made a dash for it, screaming that we were going to miss the bus. It worked. We just got the bus by the skin of our teeth; so Jemma got off at her stop at Blackhall and Billy got on at the stop after. When Billy saw me all geared up for the occasion he looked a bit put out and he said, Oh, can we go to the disco later on? Sure, I said, I'll do anything. So we went right through Bucksburn on the bus, past all the shops, and we didn't get off till we were right on the outskirts.

It was a really weird place – some kind of industrial estate, I suppose. I've seen it lots of times before, going past, but I've never been close to it like that. It's all these horrible huge long buildings with no windows. We stopped in front of one. It had spotlights trained on the front of it; like big, long, silver fingers, it made the place look spooky. There was a little glass building, like a square glass box, stuck onto the front of the sheds. It had lights on – there was someone in it, I think: but the main building didn't show any lights at all. That's the place, Billy said. That's where it started from. He meant on the night of the accident – though it can't have been where *he* actually started from, I mean, where he actually started from must have been away up at that hut where Grandad lived in the summertime. Maybe he meant that's where his memory started – or where he lost his memory? I'm still not sure how much he does remember – maybe it's more than he lets on. Anyway I was so busy look-ing at the way the beams of light crossed each other and made strange pools and shad-ows and spiky shapes on the grass in front of the building, I forgot to look at the name of the place – then afterwards I forgot to ask him what it was. I can't see it matters much anyway.

He started to walk away from it. I said, Is that all you want to do here? and he said yes. There was a really cold wind that kept blow-ing down the spaces between the buildings, and it kept blowing the bottom of my coat open and my legs were freezing. Billy just had his denim jacket and jeans on, *as always*,

and his sandshoes, and I asked him was he
cold, and he said no, it didn't bother him.
But he never asked me if I was cold. I was
beginning to feel very sorry for myself. I
thought, Gosh, he doesn't care for anyone
except himself, what am I doing walking
around this awful place with him? A ghost
town. Did you have a good time on Friday
night, Treeza? Oh yes, I had a lovely time; I
walked all round an industrial estate with
Billy Stuart, it was really good, I got frostbite
in my knees and an icicle on the end of my
nose and it was just so incredibly romantic.

Then I slipped my arm into his. He turned
and looked at me, I think he was a bit surprised. Yes, I'm here! And we walked on like
that till we came back into the town. When
we got into the streets and there were people
about, I took my arm out again. I don't
know why – perhaps I thought he'd be
embarrassed. But – it was amazing – he
stopped and turned and looked at me and
said, I liked that. My heart rate went up to
double! I pretended I hadn't understood, and
said, What? He said, Walking like that, with
your arm there. I just about dropped dead. I
smiled, I think I must have looked all coy. He
said, I'm hungry – do you want to go to the
disco or do you just want to go into that
chipper? I thought, Oh, great – all geared up,
endured frozen knees and the loss of four

toes, and why? Just so I can grace the chipper
in Bucksburn. But Muggins doesn't complain: all I said was, All right, if you want. So
we sat in there for a bit and we had chips
and we played a few records on the jukebox,
and we talked a bit about – guess who?
Geordie.

It was a strange friendship: they were
always just on the edge of quarrelling, but
they could never quite do without each other.
I don't even know if they thought of themselves as friends. I think Drift changed everything anyway. There was some stupid quarrel
and they stopped talking. And then I came
along. But I can see that Billy misses Geordie
now, a lot.

At one stage I said, Do you want to go to
the disco? He said, I don't really know what
it's like. It's funny: when he first asked if I
wanted to go to Bucksburn – back at the
beginning of the winter – he seemed, for a
moment, quite the man of the world. I sort of
got the impression he'd been there lots of
times before – I mean, I knew perfectly well
it wasn't like him, but I just had this image.
Now, when I looked at him I just thought, he
just looks totally woebegone, he looks just
like a little boy – maybe even just a puppy,
and I suddenly got this flood of really tender
feeling towards him. I really am an idiot, I
can't control my emotions at all.

His hand was lying on the table. It was
Formica – the table I mean, not his hand –
with a crazy pattern all over it that you could
go on looking at for hours (I was tracing the
pattern with my finger) and still never make
any sense of. He'd really washed his hands
well for a change, there wasn't even any dirt
under his nails. I said, Have you had a bath?
He smiled, and nodded, sort of sheepish. I
said, Was that for me? And he went all red! I
said, Was it? louder, and kicked him under
the table. He just muttered something and
started picking up crumbs of chips out of his
plate. I said, Stop it: and when he didn't I
slapped his hand – but it was a very gentle
slap! Then I took hold of his hand and laid it
down on the table, and laid my own hand
down next to it. He didn't move his hand. I
said, Do you miss Geordie? He shrugged. I
said, I used to be quite friendly with him. He
said, I know. I said, Did you ever talk about
me? No, he said, not really. What does not
really mean? I said. He said, We didn't talk
about you at all. Charming, I said.

We didn't say anything more for a bit, but
our hands were still on the table, so I said,
Look how much bigger your hand is than
mine, but my fingers look much longer and
thinner than yours. He grunted. Then I put
my hand closer to his, I put my pinkie on top
of his pinkie. That was too much for him – I

did it! I did it! He actually put his hand on
top of mine and held it! I looked up at him,
and he looked at me. And he was – different:
it was almost like something had cracked
inside him. There's something really hard
and tough inside him, and at that moment it
suddenly seemed to have softened, or even
cracked. Because of me touching him. He
didn't look like a boy any more. I suppose he
didn't look like a man either, but he looked
more like a man than a boy. I turned my
hand over under his, and we started tickling
each other's wrists with our fingertips. Suddenly I thought, supposing someone comes in
here that knows me, and sees me doing this –
someone that knows Mum and Dad. So I
leaped up and said, Let's go for a walk. I
didn't mind the thought of cold knees compared with how awful it would be if someone
came in and saw us.

When we got outside, I found I didn't
want to go to the disco anyway. I think we
both wanted to go on from where we'd left
off in the café. As we walked up the street I
slipped my arm into his again, then slid my
hand down to his. It was in his jacket pocket.
He took his hand out of his pocket and held
my hand. He held my hand! It felt a bit awkward, but really nice. There was a little street
off to the left and we went up it. I don't
know why, we just did. It went into a little

115

square of old houses, some of them were just cottages really with gardens in front of them. And there was this bit of wall, not near any of the houses and not near any of the street-lights – but not too far away from them either. And there was no wind there – it felt: just right. It was the right place. We just stopped there, both together by the wall. His whole face looked different because the lights were dim: his eyes were all deep and dark and he looked much older.

Well, we kissed, and that. We held each other. It was too good to write about. Well, it wasn't *that* good, it was a bit uncomfortable really, because he seemed all bony and awkward, and I think he felt there were some places where he shouldn't touch me. (Don't Touch Girls There Because They Might *Explode*!) But – no, I don't want to write about it. It was satisfying. Thinking about it, writing about it, it's become really, really good.

When he got off the bus in Blackhall I felt like I was in a dream. Jemma teased me stupid after she got on and I was sitting there like a zombie.

February 9th, 1974

Oh, well. I suppose it had to happen sooner

or later. Billy and I quarrelled. It was last Wednesday and we haven't spoken since. It wasn't about anything important. I can't even be bothered writing about it. But what it came down to was something important.

I don't mean about apologizing, even that isn't important, not *in itself*. I know I got onto him about never saying sorry to me, even when he's in the wrong, which he *often* is. I mean, it was when I started getting on to him about that that the quarrel started to turn serious.

I can see now that what we were *really* quarrelling about was the fact that I have to follow him about and sort of hang on him all the time while he's just thinking about himself – his Big Problem, Drift, the accident, Dave Simmers – he's obsessed.

I suppose I encouraged him to be obsessed. I suppose it was me that told him he had to find himself, remember the things he'd forgotten and all that. Well, it doesn't mean he had to be *that* obsessed with it all. I'd begun to feel I was like a doll or a puppy or something that always got carted around (shades of "River Deep, Mountain High"?) – yes, I suppose you do love a doll or a puppy *in a way*, but... No – well, you love them properly, but you still just love them because they're like, well, another bit of *you*, you like them when you're doing something, but they

don't actually do anything of their own. Billy
Stuart's puppy – Billy Stuart's little bitch –
that's what I'd have been in the end, wagging
my tail and waiting for him to come and
scratch my tummy while he sat with a far-
away look in his eyes and concentrated on –

Yes, anyway, what is it he thinks about? I
mean, after all this talking about "what happened" and what he's going to do next and
all that – what's it all for? I don't suppose
he's really interested in finding out what he's
forgotten – if he was *that* interested in it he
wouldn't have forgotten it in the first place.
No, I think the whole thing's just a big cheat
to get Treeza to run around after him with
her tongue hanging out and her knees frozen
and say ooh and ah and how grand and dark
and mysterious you are, Billy Stuart, and
how I wish only to gaze at you as you forge
forward into the Unknown. Well, he's not,
and he can't even kiss properly.

That's not true. Well, it is, but I'm sure he
was getting better. And we didn't just talk
about him. And we had a lot of good times
together. And he has got beautiful eyes. And
he scrubbed his fingernails just for me.
(Once.) But I don't know – it was true, all
the same, under the surface. Maybe I *wanted*
him to be grand and dark and mysterious,
but I got to know him too well and he wasn't
grand and dark and mysterious enough.

I can still feel his arms round me. Geordie felt sort of – better: but you somehow knew, with him, it couldn't get any better. With Billy, I sort of feel – felt, rather – he'll change, it could become really wonderful, sometime.

Maybe he didn't kiss me because he really wanted to. Maybe it was just because he felt that that was what was expected of him. Well I never *expected* him to. I wanted him to, but I didn't *expect* it.

I suppose I don't really know him that well, after all. I suppose if I was going to get to know him really well he'd have been able to come to my house and everything would be relaxed, and I'd be able to see what he looked like against the background of every-thing I know, everything I've lived with all my life. I think that's the only way you can really get to know a person properly. I don't know anything about his Saturday nights – playing with the fruit machine (I've never played a fruit machine, you're not even sup-posed to if you're under eighteen) or playing darts or talking about motorbikes and cars with the other boys from the village. And I've never been in a pub either: I don't even know what the inside of a pub looks like, except that there's a lot of smoke and the lights always look dim.

The gap's too wide. I'll never get close

enough. Even if I wanted to, I mean, even if it wasn't too late.

February 20th, 1974

Two weeks now. Maybe I'll stop keeping this diary altogether.

CHAPTER
5

CONFLICT

Billy never questioned Dave Simmers' command. He kept his mouth shut. He had a story ready to account for the state of himself and his clothes when he got back home. What he could not account for was Drift's absence.

He had not reckoned on that: he had been certain that Drift would have bolted home. Not very heroic, but very understandable. But he was not at home, and Billy spent all afternoon in a frenzy searching for him but without daring to ask anyone. He didn't want people to know his dog was on the loose, especially when lambs were in the fields.

Returning from a fourth search about six o'clock that evening, he found Drift lying nervously in the garden. When he got to him, the dog rolled over onto his back, his tail curled between his legs, the living embodiment of an apology. He was clarted with dried mud and

121

had a deep gash in the pad of his left forepaw. It was still bleeding: he had been licking it.

"Where have you been, Drift?" Billy said as he knelt beside him. "What have you done?"

Drift allowed Billy to take hold of his paw, but winced and drew it away if he put pressure on it. The wound was clean, probably made by a piece of broken glass. He would have found enough of that anywhere on the railway track, or on any of the numerous rubbish dumps around.

Billy slipped into the bathroom, where his mother had a drawer of old shirts and blouses. It was Saturday night, his mother and Liz were too busy with make-up and mirrors to take any notice of him. He tore a strip off a white nylon shirt and went out with it to Drift. Then he bound the dog's paw, tried unsuccessfully to tie the bandage, undid it again and went to find a safety-pin to secure it with. When he had got it secure, he went to fetch Drift's food from the sack of meal in the porch; but when he came back Drift had pulled the bandage off again. Billy re-bound and re-secured it while Drift looked on detachedly.

He went back into the house after his mother and sister had gone. Drift followed him.

"I don't want to go to the Bridge tonight," he told his father.

His father looked surprised. "How not?"

Billy decided to come clean. "Drift's cut his foot," he said, "and I want to see he doesn't take the bandage off again."

Will Stuart frowned. This was a break with tradition. On the other hand, he was thinking, Billy was growing up. His mother had always insisted that someone should be there for him when she went to her Bingo on Saturday; that was why he had always been taken to the Bridge Bar. But surely, he was old enough by now... Besides, who had arranged for him to get the dog in the first place? Billy was only showing a sense of responsibility. Will Stuart took a deep breath.

"All right," he said. "I'll just go up with Rob." They looked at each other for an instant, two pairs of piercing blue eyes. His father winked. Billy smiled.

"You'd better not keep him in here though," his father said, "or your mother'll have something to say." He nodded towards Drift's foot: blood had already soaked through the bandage. "Try and keep his foot up," he added; "that'll stop the bleeding."

Billy took Drift out into the garden. The night was mild and still. The moon was nearly full, and was shining broad and benign in the eastern sky. Billy found a sack and folded it small and bulky. He made Drift lie down on the drying-green and put the folded sack under the wounded paw so that it was well raised.

123

Then he sat down beside him and held the paw on the sack.

It was very still. Once, a group of oyster-catchers passed overhead unseen, emitting their regular, electronic-sounding bleeps far into the distance. The moonlight bathed the boy and the dog on the small drying-green. Billy felt the warmth of Drift's body seep over him and into him. The moon rose higher across the sky, but time stood still. Everything seemed to be gathered up into a single moment that never changed. The moon rushed through space, and yet always remained overhead. Billy found himself looking dispassionately, almost benignly, back on all that had happened that day. The world was a cruel place, and there was no fighting its cruelty, and friendships were flimsy things. But somehow it ceased to matter: cruelty and friendlessness seemed to be taken up, transformed and made meaningless in that drifting silver light. Great cloudy shapes moved high up there, silver giants and shadowy beasts from a remote but more significant world. And all the while boy and dog remained motionless below in the silver basin of the garden, neither moving their heads nor making any sound, while hour followed hour.

Drift's paw became infected. The vet said the bandage had kept out the air so that the wound had festered. He cleaned it out, then cut ragged edges in the healed flesh and stitched the gash together. Drift limped around for two weeks, and Billy kept a close eye on him.

His escapade had not gone unnoticed. Jimmy Wilson, the neighbouring farmer, had seen him, and warned Billy's father not to let the dog stray.

But Billy soon discovered that the damage was already done.

Shortly before his paw had completely healed, Drift sneaked away on his own, one day when Billy was at school. When Billy returned in the afternoon, there was no Drift again. It was like a stab in the back. No one knew where he had been or which way he had gone; but Billy saw him skulking back about eight o'clock that night, skirting the edges of Jimmy Wilson's fields, always keeping close to the fence.

"Keep him without his supper," his father said, "and shut him up in the shed."

"But he's to have his supper!" Billy protested.

"Not if he goes off like that." His father was adamant, and watched from the house while Billy took Drift down to the shed and latched the door.

Drift howled all night. Billy had intended letting him out in the night and feeding him, but he was afraid it would only arouse his father's suspicions if the howling stopped suddenly.

"Where does he go?" Billy asked.

"He'll just be raking around," his father said. "Eating rubbish, or chasing rabbits. But it's the lambs that are the trouble."

"Drift wouldn't kill lambs!" Billy said fiercely. "He'd never do it!"

"You never know," his father said.

Billy now doubled the time he went out with Drift in the evenings. He ranged all over the hill of Craigmore, once even to within distant sight of the tall trees round Peter Ward's hut. He would walk back all the way from the Yard because his father would have given up waiting for him. His mother began to complain that he wasn't getting enough sleep.

What he found hardest to take was the fact that, although the bond between himself and Drift seemed closer week by week, nothing he could say or do seemed able to break Drift of his new habit. It was as though Dave Simmers' boot had altered his whole make-up. Billy could still make him lie down, run on, walk to heel, without even having to use a word or a whistle, almost as though he commanded the dog by a kind of telepathy. But what he could not do was make him stay at home when he himself was not there. Whenever he was shut up in the shed, Drift howled. At one moment,

126

Billy felt betrayed; at the next, he felt he was betraying the dog by going away. How could Drift understand why Billy had to go to school?

It was on the school bus home one Friday night that Billy saw Drift. They were still three or four miles away from Davieburn by the road, which at that point crossed over the old railway track. The bus made a wide loop up towards Falkirk, and then wound back on a minor road towards Davieburn, but the railway track went from Blackhall to Davieburn in a single sweeping curve. Billy glanced up towards the village as they went over the bridge. The railway track went through a deep cutting here. The sun had found a chink in the silvery clouds and was filling the cutting with palest gold, lighting up the vivid greens on the banks and picking out the bright yellow flowers dotted in the cinders of the track itself. And there was Drift, a flamboyant splash of ruddy brown among the fresh spring colours. He had just come off one of the steep banks onto the track, and was ambling down towards the bridge, moving slowly, stopping, sniffing, just an idle dog having an idle afternoon's amusement.

Suddenly Billy felt angry. The bus stopped just after that to let a girl off to one of the farms. Billy jumped up from his seat, pushed forward with his jacket and his bag, and slithered off just behind her. He heard some laughing in the bus behind him, but didn't stop to think what it meant: all he was aware of was his anger at Drift. How could he! When he must know that Billy was on his way home, how could he simply wander off and spend the afternoon sniffing around!

The girl looked round, startled. She was called Theresa Thain. Billy didn't know her to speak to. She didn't turn away, but stood looking at Billy questioningly. There was no one but the two of them on an empty road. Billy was arrested: Drift was uppermost in his mind, but something prevented him putting his head down and walking straight off when she was looking at him like that. She had round, grey eyes and fine, regular eyebrows. As the bus drew away she smiled. Billy flushed and hitched his schoolbag strap onto his shoulder, thumping the bag round behind him with clumsy energy.

"Are you *walking* home tonight?" she said. Her smile was amused, but uncertain. Her eyes grew rounder, her eyebrows arching a little. The sun was making lights in her fine brown hair.

Billy wrenched himself. "Aye," he said gruffly, then put his head down and turned sharply back towards the bridge. After he had gone a few steps he realized that he was dragging his jacket along the ground behind him.

128

That was stupid. None of his limbs felt as if they were working properly. He was stiff and clumsy. He didn't look back.

He felt completely thrown: irritated, savage. When he came to the railway bridge and looked over, it was fully thirty seconds before he even realized he was looking at Drift. Then all his irritation centred on the dog. Drift was just crossing under the bridge. Billy leaned over. "Drift!" he called, his voice imperious. "What – what do you think you're doing down there?" He had been going to use a lot of swear-words, but he was held back by a stupid feeling that the girl was just behind him. It was one thing swearing in front of girls, in company, at school: but alone, on an empty road, was another.

Drift looked up. The face that looked into Billy's was the face of a stranger. For a moment Billy was in genuine doubt whether this was his own dog, the dog he walked with and fed and petted every day, that understood his every thought and move. Could there be another dog like Drift? This dog's eyes were wild and wicked.

"Drift," he called, more softly; "Drift, come here." But Drift's tail went down and he turned and bolted up the track towards Davieburn. Billy ran back to the end of the bridge. He glanced up the road, registered a moment's surprise – a moment's emptiness –

that the girl was no longer there, then scrambled over the parapet and skidded down the cutting to the old track.

Horsetail and coltsfoot overgrew much of the cinders and gravel, but here and there pieces of broken glass glinted up in the wan sunlight. Billy gave chase to Drift, calling out his name until he was breathless. But when Drift looked back and saw Billy following, he dived up the embankment and under the fence and Billy lost sight of him.

It was years since Billy had cried about anything; but standing on the top of the embankment with his hands on the sagging fence-wire, looking out over the quiet fields empty of Drift, he was blinded by tears of sheer frustration.

"When I get home," he muttered, "I'll thrash him. I called to him and he didn't come. I'm going to get a stick and I'm going to thrash him."

But Drift was not at home. Billy threw his jacket and schoolbag down on the kitchen floor. When his mother told him to put them away, he kicked them into a corner and stormed out.

He had barely got outside when Andy Gibbon's scarlet BMW came wavering slowly round the corner and stopped outside their house. It sat there for almost five minutes before anyone got out. Andy Gibbon kept the car spotlessly clean, and it looked odd somehow, sitting there so polished, so garish, so expensive among the small second-hand cars and vans between the rows of drab council houses on either side of the street.

The door opened eventually and Andy Gibbon climbed out. He leaned heavily on the car for support, and seemed to have a lot of difficulty finding the garden gate. He was very red in the face and very drunk. He didn't notice Billy. He half knocked at the front door and then half fell in.

Billy mooched. He wanted to look for Drift and he didn't want to look for him. I hope he's caught chasing lambs and gets shot, he thought; and as soon as he had thought it he tried to un-think it again, in case Someone heard him and took him at his word.

The front door opened. "Would you come here, Billy?" It was his mother, harassed, amused, conspiratorial.

Billy went in. His mother whispered in the hall, "It's Andy. He's just completely past it. He's wanting to speak to your father, he says."

"What's to stop him?"

She grimaced. "He's probably in the same state himself. They've been up at the Bridge all afternoon. I think Andy meant to go back up there just now, but he couldn't make it so he came here instead. Just as well, for I saw the bobbies going through the village just back

131

there. I don't know what to do with him."

"Do you want me to go and get Dad?" Billy suggested. "I could go on my bike."

His mother thought. "Well – you could. But he mustn't drive back down if he's in that state. You could get Fergus to bring him down, he'd do that for you." Fergus was the chef at the Bridge Restaurant.

"I'll get my jacket," Billy said, and went into the kitchen. Andy Gibbon was there, sitting at the kitchen table, his head resting on it, his arms sprawled across it with his wide, red hands drooping over the far edge. He had on his baggiest, oiliest, working jersey and trousers, a strange contrast to the car he had just got out of. When Billy came in he raised himself on his elbows.

"Where's your dad?" he mumbled. His eyes looked watery, and his flushed cheeks were wet. He looked for all the world as if he had been crying.

"I'm just going to get him," Billy said, picking up his jacket.

"You do that, son. You just do that." There was a definite catch in his voice. "I want to speak to him. You should always speak, you shouldn't stop speaking. You and my Geordie – you and my Geordie, now..." He stopped and looked around vacantly: he had lost his thread.

Billy saw, to his amazement, that Andy

132

Gibbon *had* been crying. He was on the verge of tears now. Billy looked at his mother as she came in, but as soon as he caught her eye she quickly turned away, clearly suppressing a fit of giggles.

"He's such a bloody fool," Andy Gibbon sobbed. "I'm only wanting the best for him, Beth. I love that man. I love him like a brother. But he's such a bloody fool. Look at you here, Beth, just look at you! But he can't see his way to anything better. I'm just trying to widen his horizons, that's all I'm trying to do. I don't want the partnership broken up." Tears were streaming down his face.

"Billy's just away for Will now, Andy," Billy's mother said. "He'll not be long. Just you sit there now and keep quiet. Why, you're in an awful state!"

Billy went out full of the image of Andy Gibbon, sitting at the table with his arms stretched out, his hands palm upwards, as if in supplication to his mother.

He pulled his bike out of the shed and rode as fast as he could up the hill out of Davieburn, and then down along the Avenue. He didn't ride fast out of any feeling of urgency, but because riding fast gave him something to do that took up his energy. Riding till his breath came in gasps and the wind hammered in his ears, he didn't have to think or feel anything.

There were a few cars and vans parked at

the Bridge already, his father's among them. It was only just after opening-time, but obviously the Bridge had been unofficially open all afternoon. That did happen occasionally. It normally meant the police had visited within the last few days, so that no further visits would be expected for the next couple of weeks.

Billy saw his father as soon as he went in. He was sitting relaxed but upright at the bar, with a glass of solid black liquid in front of him. Billy supposed it was sweet stout, which was what his father drank when he wanted to sober himself up. He didn't look entirely sober, but he was certainly in nothing like the state that Andy Gibbon was in. Dod Moffat was humped at the end of the bar, looking as if he were attached to it in some mysterious, organic way. He had taken his cap off, and the wisps of grey hair on either side of his bald crown were sticking almost straight out. Dod Moffat would rub the sides of his head furiously when he was drinking hard. It was the only sign that he was very drunk indeed.

Dave Simmers was there as well. Billy was taken aback at this, since his white van had not been outside. He wondered if he had come there with Andy Gibbon. He avoided looking in his direction. There were a few others too, workers from the glassworks who hadn't been able to wait till the end of the week and had taken Friday off.

Billy gave his message to his father, who immediately left his stool and his drink, nodded affably to Dod Moffat and Hettie, the barmaid, and went out.

Billy turned to go, but Hettie called after him to nip over to the kitchen and pick up a couple of boxes of crisps from Fergus. It was something Billy occasionally did for her, and she would give him a few packets of crisps in return. He didn't feel like crisps at that moment, but he could hardly refuse. He ducked under the bar hatch, made his way through the dim, unlit lounge, down the steps to the cellar, where the big steel kegs stood silent and gleaming in the half-darkness; and along the concrete-floored passage to the kitchen.

"Is Dod Moffat still there?" was the first thing Fergus asked him when he got there.

"He's sitting at the bar," Billy said.

Fergus seemed anxious. "He's in a foul humour," he said. "It'd be better to get him home for his tea."

"He was quiet when I went in," Billy said.

Fergus rooted and shuffled among the boxes and packages in the kitchen store but couldn't find what Hettie had asked for. "I've got salt and vinegar, barbecue chicken, beef and tomato and cheese and onion," he said, "but I've no gammon."

"I'll just take the plain," Billy said. He felt impatient. There was nothing he particularly wanted to do, and he had been keen enough to get away from the house before: but now that he was away, he wanted to get back.

"I'll have a look over here in this lot," Fergus said. And Billy had to stand for another five minutes clutching the box of plain crisps, until Fergus was fully satisfied that he had nothing else.

As Billy came up the cellar steps into the lounge, he heard shouting through from the public bar. He went more slowly, apprehensively.

Hettie was not behind the bar, nor was Dod Moffat in his place. Everyone seemed crowded over at the door. Billy put the box of crisps on the bar and then went through the bar hatch to see what was happening. He noticed Dod Moffat's cap lying on the floor.

Hettie and one of the other men were shouting – not arguing, but trying to calm people down. Then Billy saw that the man was hanging onto Dave Simmers by the arm. Blood was streaming from Dave Simmers' nose. All at once he jerked his arm free from the man's hold, and lunged forward at Dod Moffat, who was immediately in front of him. He struck for the old farmer's chest, but from too far back, for he missed his aim and was again grabbed from behind and held. Dod Moffat roared something incomprehensible at him, his normal husky growl distorted with anger. It was obvious Dave Simmers was not keen to get too close to Dod Moffat's fist again.

"You just try it! You just try it!" Dave Simmers yelled, almost in a scream. "You see what happens!"

"Aye, you'd squeal," Dod Moffat growled, "you backside-foremost little runt. You'd squeal like the dirty little rat you are." He stepped forward towards Dave Simmers. His bulging belly looked like solid rock.

Hettie stepped in front of him. "If you hit him again, Dod Moffat," she said, "I'll ban you. I mean it. I'll not let you back in here."

For a moment Dod Moffat glowered at her, smouldering. Then suddenly his grey flushed face relaxed, and his mouth broke into its huge, thin-lipped grin. "Give us a kiss, darling," he said.

The crisis was over. Dod Moffat was escorted over to his elderly van, and Dave Simmers, with a little more fuss, set walking down the road towards the Avenue. Billy picked up Dod's cap and ran outside with it to hand through the open van door. Dod grinned down at him benignly. Billy fetched his bike, and followed the old yellow van's stately progress all round the long road past the Bing, until it turned off onto the hill-road up to Craigmore and Billy continued on towards

Davieburn. He had avoided the Avenue, having no wish to overtake Dave Simmers.

Andy Gibbon had left before Will Stuart arrived. When Billy got back, both his father and mother were shaking their heads and laughing over the partner's behaviour.

"Where's your dog?" his father asked as Billy came in.

"He was on the railway line," Billy answered, evasively. He looked out of the kitchen window. "He's back now," he added. Drift was lying half on his side on the back green, looking anxiously towards the window.

"He gave me the slip," Billy's mother put in, "just after dinner-time. He's been away all that time."

"Right," his father said, getting up decisively. "Right, he's got to be taught a lesson. Where's that choker of Rob's, Billy?"

Billy fetched the choker. "What are you going to do, Dad?"

"I said: I'm going to teach him a lesson. You needn't watch if you don't want to."

Billy followed, a knot in the pit of his stomach.

His father put the choker on Drift and led him to the shed. Billy noticed his father didn't look at Drift at all. There was something ominous about his calm, unfocussed gaze into the distance.

There was a stick of tough seasoned hazelwood standing against the shed wall. Billy's father picked it up.

"Dad, you're not going to hit him with the stick?"

"He's got to learn, Billy."

"Dad, please!"

"Just keep away now." Drift crouched there, tense, goggle-eyed. He seemed almost, but not quite, to realize what was going to happen. Billy's father gripped the leash in his left hand, and with the other brought the stick whistling down onto Drift's haunch. Then the dog realized. He leaped up, twisting round on the leash, letting out a horrible, screaming yell.

"Dad, no!" Billy covered his ears with his hands.

Again the whistle and again the yell. And again. Drift was leaping and writhing so much he was choking on the leash. It seemed to anger Billy's father, because he started shouting something, adding to the din. Drift's yelling grew harsh and gurgling; foam flecked his mouth.

Billy ran forwards and gripped his father's arm. His father turned. Drift sat hunched, trembling, gasping for breath. "Dad, can you not see," Billy screamed, "that'll just make him worse! It will! He'll never want to come back if he thinks he's going to get that!"

His father shook him off, and again raised the stick. All Drift's yelling had been for three

139

strokes, no more.

"Go inside," Will Stuart said. "Get inside, and stay there. Go on!" And he struck again, and again the dog's yelling started.

Billy fled, bent as he ran, almost as if to ward off blows to himself. He rushed into the house, up to his room, threw himself onto the bed, stuffed the blankets into his ears. For the second time that day he burst into tears – frustration and anger had given way now to grief, pain, bewilderment.

For a whole three weeks after that, Drift made no attempt to run away.

Package 7

Hobart
July 17, 1984

Dear Roger,

I'm breaking the rules this time,
because the next bit of my diary is a
bit I don't really want to send you, so
I won't. I went through a "stage" after
Billy Stuart and I stopped talking - it
was all linked up with Geordie Gibbon
going away too. I think between the two
of them they'd helped to keep me a
fairly reasonable person. Be that as it
may, the next two or three entries of
my diary are about my exploits during
the time when I didn't have either of
them - three months, to be exact. The
Tales of Treeza the Teenage Sexpot. It
isn't particularly interesting - I
mean, nothing really *happened* - but I
don't want anyone reading it because
it's plain embarrassing, even now. I
was very silly. I don't mean I did anything "stupid" - I was just silly. I
did chop and change quite a lot with
boys (including the dreaded Ally
Gordon, who was utterly pathetic),

which, I suppose, did get me a bit of a
reputation at school, but the whole
reason I did chop and change was
because nothing was very satisfactory.

As far as satisfaction went, I got
far more out of being with clumsy,
bony, messed-up Billy Stuart, though I
don't think I realized it at the time.

By the way – yes, I did read your
letter, and just in case you've forgotten: *I don't want you making comments
until you've got the last chapter.* I
know I mentioned something about you
making a response, but I meant your
eventual response. Anyway, I think I
was totally fair in how I depicted that
famous First Encounter. What's "no
small opinion of yourself" supposed to
mean, anyway? I was fair both to what
actually happened and to myself: he did
run into me when he got off the bus
that day; I did confuse him – though
not half as much as he confused me! –
and I think it was only fair to
describe me as he would have seen me: I
did it from some old photos of me, if
you must know. Perhaps your own memory
might stretch back to the nice-looking
young thing I was then.

OK? Now that's your last warning.

T.T.

CHAPTER
6

THE PLACE

Uncle Bill had died. Uncle Bill was Billy's father's uncle who had lived, and died, and was to be buried, in Fife.

Billy's father bolted the old bus seat into the back of the van, and his mother put carpet squares down on the floor. There was room for the five of them, and a little space in the back, so Billy assumed Drift would be going too. When he was told that this wouldn't be at all proper at a funeral and Drift would have to stay at home, he threatened not to go with them. When his mother told him that was all right, he could stay at home if he wanted and look after himself, Billy quickly got cold feet. His mother and Liz teased him about it, and he accepted their teasing phlegmatically, as men did.

Drift would just have to stay with the greyhound for the two days and two nights they were to be away, and Mrs MacIntosh from next-door-but-one would feed them. Mrs MacIntosh had looked after the greyhound before. The shed had two doors: the two dogs were to be tied up at opposite ends of it so that they wouldn't get their chains tangled up, and they would be able to go in and out as they wanted.

They left on Friday evening. From Friday night until Sunday lunchtime the family reunion gathered momentum, with its quarrels, reconciliations, and well-worn jokes freshly brought out for the occasion. They were within sight of the sea, but they never had time to go down to it. Billy wondered how Drift would have reacted to the sea. Burnwater fascinated and maddened him, and he might stand in it half an hour at a stretch, vainly trying to snatch at it with his teeth.

Dusk was falling as they returned on Sunday. Billy ran to the back garden before he even went into the house. The greyhound sat bolt upright in front of the shed, like a bronze ornament. There was no sign of Drift. "Drift, Drift, come on!" Billy called as he went across the green. The greyhound got up and wagged her tail but there was no movement from the other end of the shed.

Drift's chain was lying on the grass. It was still secured at the shed end; but at the other, the end link was torn open.

144

"Well," Mrs MacIntosh said, "he broke loose on the Saturday, though goodness only knows how; that's when I found him gone. But he was back there next morning – this morning, that is. I was going to tie him up, but he looked that happy just sitting there I thought, well, just let him be. I didn't think he'd go off again. I'm sure he'll be back soon."

By midnight that night, the whole household was silent in bed. Billy waited another full half-hour. Then softly, softly so that even he could not hear his own movements below Rob's gentle snoring, he crept out of his room. The fourth stair creaked. Billy took a large step over it. He found his father's torch in the drawer of the kitchen table without even having to turn the light on, then slipped out of the back door and clicked it gently to behind him.

The sky was overcast, with a smur of rain, but faint moonlight suffused the night through the clouds. Billy ran straight to the old railway track. He followed it down for over two miles, further than the bridge where it crossed under the main road. He flicked the torch occasionally, occasionally climbed to the tops of the cuttings, and called and whistled softly. He walked further than he had ever done down the track, but there was no sign, no sound of trotting feet, nothing but the buzz, now and then, of a night-travelling lorry to break the silence of the night and the soft hush of the rain on the fields, the soft patter of the rain on his jacket. His hair hung lank and dripping round his ears and forehead.

He came back to Davieburn by the road. Then he turned off and walked halfway up Culane Hill. He returned to the railway track and followed back through the village, then took the shortest way over-field to Craigmore, and climbed in the night until he lost all notion of how far he had gone. Everywhere it was the same: blank, rain-hushed silence, broken only once by two swift reports of a shotgun from away ahead up the hill. That gave Billy no particular concern on Drift's account, because it could only come from one source. But he quickly turned back: he had no wish to meet Peter Ward, hunting, at dead of night. The rain stopped about four in the morning, but by that time it had trickled down his neck and wet him inside as well as soaking through his jacket from the outside.

Daylight had imperceptibly soaked through the clouds by the time Billy found his feet were taking him home. He had not meant to go back home, ever, not until he had found Drift. But paralyzing tiredness, and the chill spreading through him from his soaking clothes, and his eyes straining wildly in every direction into the night, had together taken him near to a state of trance. He was no longer his own master: his feet took him home, his hands opened the kitchen door and put the torch back into the drawer, his feet took him up the stairs, his hands undressed him, his whole body let him collapse into bed. His mind was so much shut off from him that he forgot even to check whether Drift had come back.

His mother woke him two hours later: time for school. Billy got up automatically, dressed in his school things and went down for breakfast. He forgot to ask if Drift had come back. His mother had already checked for herself and found that he had not. She found Billy's silence strange, and looked closely at him. There was something glazed about his eyes.

"Are you all right, Billy?" she asked.

"Aye, I'm all right," he answered distractedly.

"Are you not going to eat your breakfast?" she asked.

"I'm not hungry," he said.

He seemed unaware of the time. She hustled him along, and he let himself be hustled. But when he went to unhook his jacket from its peg, he was unable to lift his arm high enough. He stood there, looking at the peg in a puzzled way. His mother found him there a few minutes later, trembling uncontrollably. Then the trembling passed and he looked at her again in that same glazed, puzzled way.

147

"Back to your bed, Billy," she said. And he went.

She took a hot-water bottle to him and found his soaking clothes from the night. She picked the clothes up but said nothing.

Later in the day when she went to see him, he said, very clearly and forcefully: "Put Drift's food out for him, Mum, so he can have it when he comes back." She said she would.

Billy's face grew flushed, and by evening he was in a high fever. He tossed and muttered all night. His mother slept beside him, in Rob's bed.

By Tuesday morning the fever had abated a little, and she decided it wasn't worth the trouble of getting the doctor out from Blackhall. Gradually through the day Billy seemed to return to himself.

On one occasion in the afternoon he suddenly sat up in bed and called out, "Mum, he's come back!" Drift had jumped through the bedroom window and landed on his bed. When his mother went up, it took her fully ten minutes to persuade him it was a dream. Billy thumped and poked the bedclothes all over before he was satisfied that Drift really had not come back; only then did he realize that not even Drift could have leaped through a first-floor window.

He felt he was coming out of a dark tunnel. The track seemed to go on endlessly – stones,

148

cinders, gleaming pieces of broken glass. Sometimes the glass was discoloured. Was that blood on it?

All the while he had lain in bed, the sun had not shone. The days had been grey and clouded, and now and then the same soft rain would fall, for three or four hours on end. By Wednesday he was allowed to get up and wander around a little. He never asked or spoke about Drift. The cloud-cover lifted, and the air was filled with a pale yellow light that was never quite sunshine.

On Wednesday evening the sun came from behind the clouds as it went down. Everything became hazy and golden, rain-washed and distinct, and midges danced in the still mild air. Billy turned his back to the sun and gazed up towards the soft golden silhouette of Culane Hill, topped by its abrupt golden nipple. His brain felt clear and fresh.

Suddenly he stiffened. He had heard something: distant, distant beyond the sound of voices in the street, cars in the village, the low-pitched wails of sheep and the rumble of lorries on the distant main road. There it was again. Was it a song he heard? No – it was like a song, but only a little. He strained, strained into the distance, as if by straining hard enough he could hear every sound between him there and the distant North Sea beyond the far tongue of Fife.

149

At last it came again, quite beyond doubt this time. It was not singing, it was a dog howling, howling down the long reach of golden air. Not where he was gazing, up towards Culane Hill, but – there, a bit to the right. Wait: and there it was again, quite clearly now, a long mournful howling, exactly over there, in a straight line over that rowan-tree. And not a shadow of doubt: that was Drift's howl, Billy could have picked it out from a whole kennelful of dogs.

"Mum!" He turned to run in, then stopped, on the point of opening the back door. Slowly he retraced his steps. What was the point in telling her? She would just think he was imagining things again. Billy went back to where he had stood before. He listened carefully for a half-hour longer, as the sun dipped and sank and all became grey, but he did not hear the howl again.

He would not be allowed out tonight, of that he was quite certain: but what difference did that make? If Drift was howling, he was shut up somewhere; and if he was shut up somewhere, tomorrow morning would be as good as tonight. And besides, he had begun to feel so tired – as if worn out by the effort of listening. He marked the direction exactly, the tree that was on the line of the howling, so that he knew precisely which way to take next morning. Then he went inside.

* * *

The sun came shining brightly into Billy's room, and tall mountainous clouds were processing grandly round the sky's horizons. Billy woke up thinking, Today I'll find him again.

As soon as he could after breakfast he went out into the garden and checked that he could make out the right tree on the wild bank that ran round the edge of Wilson's field. Then he told his mother he was going for a stroll.

The breeze was gentle; it was nearly warm enough for summer. Billy scrambled through the fence, crossed the corner of the field towards the single rowan-tree on the bank. Everything seemed new-washed and clean. He went over the fence at the far side. Larch and birch trees were in full leaf, and their fresh scent hung all around. The rowan was still stretching its long many-fingered leaves, its green soft and virginal. Billy stood beside it and looked back. There was his house, there was the green; there was the pole of the washing-line he had stood beside. He stretched out his arm, taking a line from the pole to where he stood; then stretched the other arm in the opposite direction, continuing the line. The next landmark was a cluster of trees and farm buildings a couple of miles away. There was nothing but a clump of trees between him and the farm, with the main road running through the midst of them. Billy knew the

151

farm's name, Pitmullen, but he had never been there and did not know the farmer, Sandy Thain. He decided he would have to ask there first of all. If Drift was accused of chasing sheep, accused he would have to be, even if the police were called in and a charge made. Billy felt he could cross all these bridges as he came to them: the main thing was to find Drift.

He did not cut straight across to Pitmullen. There was nowhere before there where Drift could possibly be shut up, Billy thought, so he would be best taking the quickest route. He returned to the house and fetched his bike. The old railway track was risky for his wheels because of all the broken glass, but he decided to take the risk.

He left the bike at the bridge he had crossed under three nights previously, and climbed the steep bank up onto the road. Walking along the grass verge towards the Pitmullen sign-board, he felt strangely vulnerable. The cars and lorries went by so fast, so seemingly oblivious to a single frail figure, frail flesh and blood, picking its way through tussocky grass that was never meant for walking on but was merely there to mark the edge of the road.

The farm-road up to Pitmullen had been muddy, but the sun had already been warm enough to dry long stretches of it. Here and there clay was cracked round the wide rim of puddles. He reached the farm steading and looked around for signs of life.

A kindly looking man in dungarees with a black belt and a green cap was tinkering with a tall red forage harvester. It stood in a sunny, windless corner of the close, and the man's forehead was beaded with sweat.

He straightened up. "And what can I do for you, my lad?"

"Have you seen a dog?" Billy said.

The man paused and puckered his forehead. "What kind of a dog, now?" he asked slowly.

"He's kind of brown and white," Billy said. "Reddy-brown. He's a collie. I think he's tied up somewhere."

The man looked at him thoughtfully for a moment. "Well, I've seen him," he said eventually. "But he's dead."

There was something quiet and final in the way he said it.

"Dead?" Billy repeated. The man had shot him, because no one had come to claim him. If he had only come last night instead of waiting till the morning...

"Was it your dog?" the man said, quietly as before.

"No," said Billy. "I mean – yes." His first instinct was to deny: partly from caution, in case of a charge of sheep-worrying – but partly also because, as long as he had that name Drift in his mind, in his mouth, there seemed no possibility that Drift and the dead dog could be

153

the same. "He's been gone these three days," he said. There was a lump coming in his throat.

"I found him by the side of the road," the man said, "the day before yesterday. There wasn't a mark on him, but he was dead. The motors go at some speed along that road though. I buried him there."

"Could I go and look?" Billy said, half in a dream.

"I think there's a shovel," the man said, "leaning against the dyke round the corner there. You can take it. Go along that road there" – he pointed to another track leading out of the steading between low stone walls – "and it'll bring you out in a wee wood by the roadside. You'll easy see the place I buried him in. Have a look anyway, it'll set your mind at rest."

There's no way, Billy was thinking, it could be Drift, because he had heard the howling. But he did as the man suggested. His heart was beating a little fast, and there was an anxious knot in his stomach. Nevertheless he was as certain as he could be about anything that it was Drift he had heard the night before.

He reached the wood the farmer had described. The track soon came out into a clearing in the middle of it. On one side the wood was only a couple of trees deep, and he could see cars flashing by on the main road, strangely remote. On the far side of the road the wood continued. It was a wonderfully quiet spot, with its bright grass, grey-blue pines with their luminous red-brown trunks, dazzling larch-green, and the green-gold sheen against the sky of newly opened beech-leaves. The sunlight was gathered in a pool on the grassy floor, the breeze dappling it in silver shadows where it slanted steeply through the branches of the trees.

There was a bare patch of earth near the centre of the clearing, mounded up slightly, with two largish stones on it. It was the only possible place. Billy moved the two stones off and began to dig.

The shovel was unwieldy: a spade would have been better. It was heavy for Billy, and kept turning on stones and divots that had been raked into the hole higgledy-piggledy when it had been filled in.

He came to three larger stones protruding through the loose earth. He put down the shovel, gripped them one by one, and with a little difficulty slid them out of the soil around them. The second one revealed a dog's nose, the same pinky-brown as Drift's. The third one revealed the whole head. Dark-brown and white, the wrong colour. An eye open, dull pale brown. The teeth bared on one side, but without the puckering of the nose that would have made it a snarl.

Billy would not believe it was Drift. He half-averted his eyes, picked up the shovel, and went on digging down.

The dog had been dropped into the hole half on the vertical, with the head uppermost. When he had cleared and scrabbled the earth away as far as the forelegs, Billy looked fully at the dead animal.

"Oh, Drift!" It burst out of him quite involuntarily, in a suppressed half-sob; but still he could not let his mind encompass the truth. The dog looked different: it was too dark, Drift was a redder brown. He dug on, with his hands now, feverishly throwing the handfuls of earth up onto the pile he had begun with the shovel.

The chest, full-boned. The unexpectedly slender hindquarters. The three-inch white tip to the tail.

The colour didn't look right because the life had gone out of him. His coat had no gloss, no vibrancy. He was a discarded thing, like a leaf discarded off a tree in the autumn. One forepaw was turned back, looking strangely relaxed, at ease. The one eye was almost fully open, and soil clung around the sunken eyeball. The soil must have pushed his lip up over his teeth on that one side; the flesh was stiff now, and Billy could not get the lip to stay down in its proper place. Drift was cold: not cold like stone, but cool rather, the same temperature as the soil itself. Billy knocked loose soil from the feathery ruff. Even the white fur was discoloured now, stained clay-yellow.

The face looked so kind and wise and old.

It was true: there was not a mark on him.

Billy looked up at the treetops in a circle round him, and the sun glancing over the top of them, silver and green and gold. The thought crossed his mind: nothing'll ever be the same again.

A spider crept onto Drift's head and over his eye. Billy gently laid two fingers on the cold hair in its path. The spider hesitated, then climbed onto the fingers, and Billy reached it over behind him, letting it fall slowly on its shining thread. The grass looked as bright and hard as jewels.

Slowly, Billy began to scrape the earth back into the hole. He covered the hindquarters and the chest, and replaced two of the bigger stones, filling in around them, softly, with more soil.

Steadily the *whoosh-whoosh* of traffic went on, on the road beyond the trees.

DIARY

May 11th, 1974

I'm horribly afraid the dreams are going to start again. For the last three nights I've gritted my teeth and willed myself not to dream; but I don't really know if it's worked. I have this feeling that I had dreams but have just chosen to forget them. I don't remember these dreams but I remember what they're *about*. It's really weird. They're always about the same thing. Billy is a murderer, and he's hunting people among the bings, but the bings go stretching off everywhere, in every direction, like a shadowy desert.

May 13th, 1974

I keep thinking about Billy. Almost all the time. I don't know what's wrong with me. My thoughts are on a kind of seesaw. One moment, I'm remembering all sorts of things about him, about *us*, and I go all warm. Next moment I have this glimpse of him like he is in the dreams which I don't remember – or that time two weeks ago when he saw me with Ally Gordon – or that time at Christmas, when he said he hated Ally, the way he said he hated him – and it's like the blood all drains out of my body and I feel almost paralyzed with fear.

May 19th, 1974

I went down the track to the wood beside the road today. I might as well admit it was because I was thinking about Billy. I can't get him out of my head.

It's been a lovely, bright, sunny day all day, really hot. I went with Mum to church in the morning.

I don't know where Drift's buried, because of course Billy's never showed me. I did ask Dad that time, but he was awful secretive about it. It must be just past the anniversary of Drift's death just now. I wonder if Dad shot him. I've never asked him direct – I don't think I could. He'd go all jokey and call me "my lass" and ruffle up my hair or something. It wouldn't mean he'd done it. It wouldn't mean he hadn't done it. It would just mean: don't come bothering me, what I use my gun for is none of your business.

It's a really quiet place. It's funny, because it's the nearest place to the main road on the whole farm, and yet it's the quietest. It's as if the quietness belonged there and the noise just didn't. There was a clump of nettles in

159

the middle of the clearing, I wondered if that
was the place Drift was buried. Nettles sometimes grow up where ground's been dis-
turbed. They were dark green and very
sting-y looking, but their leaves were all
edged round with a reddy sort of colour.

I walked round the clearing, in the sunlight, for quite a long time. It just felt good,
being alone, being quiet. I don't seem to have
been alone for ages. I've been getting really
fed up with everything, and everyone. Then
the dreams started – well, tried to start. And
now I feel something's going to change. The
warm ground smelled lovely, and so did the
trees. When you went under the trees – I
think those ones are beeches – the light went
all golden and mysterious. I had the tune of
that song on Sam's record that I used to like
– the one about the girl who had to marry
the boy of fourteen, and he was the father of
a son at fifteen, but "by the age of sixteen his
grave it was green" – going round and round
in my head, and suddenly new words came
into my head to fit the tune: "The trees are
your roof made of green and of gold." I was
quite surprised at myself. I went on humming
the tune, but no other words came, and I
started thinking about the line that had come
to me. "Your roof" meant Drift's roof, of
course, then I thought I didn't like the idea of
standing there speaking to a dead dog I'd

never met. "Dead dog" sounds *really* dead –
much deader than a dead person! So I
changed "your" to "my", and then I suddenly got a second line:

> *The trees are my roof made of green and*
>   *of gold*
> *And I think it must be where you lost your*
>   *soul...*

That must have been because of going to
church in the morning! And first of all I
thought "you" and "your" meant Drift
again, but almost immediately I knew it
wasn't: it was Billy I was meaning – he'd lost
his soul there – and suddenly I got this knot
of feeling in my stomach: it was really
painful, and then it rose up through my chest
and shoulders and into my head, and before I
knew what was happening I was standing
there with the tears streaming down my face.

   I didn't realize I actually still felt so much
for Billy. I know I've been *thinking* a lot
about him, but thinking isn't the same as
feeling.

   It wasn't just Billy, though – well, it was,
but it was me too. It seems a bit silly thinking
back to it now, but what I felt this afternoon,
as I was standing there blubbering, was that
it was *me* that had lost my soul because I
didn't have Billy any more, and that's why
I'd been acting so stupid over the past few

weeks. It *was* stupid: I haven't really enjoyed any of it – the only bits I enjoyed was giggling about it with Jemma afterwards, about what he did, and where he put his hand, and what you did next and – oh, yeugh. We always finish by saying: oh, yeugh, and falling about laughing.

It's really weird when I think that the first time I met Billy – I mean met him properly, not that time on the road, but by the Bing, when we talked about music and raspberries, and that – was just after that had happened, I mean just after Drift getting killed, and my dad burying him, in our wood. I don't know why it's weird, it just is.

Package 8

Hobart
July 31, 1984

Dear Roger,

I see there's a mention of an exam in
one of these diary entries. As far as I
can see that's the sole and only refer-
ence to "O" levels, which I was doing
that year. What can one infer from that?
    There's also another mention… Don't
take it amiss…

T.T.

CHAPTER
7

DOD MOFFAT

There were sixty-one posts along the side of the Tip, sixty-one posts between the two big corner strainers. On three sides the Yard bordered on Craigmore land, Dod Moffat's farm, and on those three sides there was a simple stob-and-wire fence. It was only on the side that ran along the road that the high steel-mesh fence had been erected, with the big padlocked gate. Dod Moffat had sold Andy Gibbon the piece of land for the Yard seven years before, when he and Will Stuart started in partnership, but the Tip had been there long before then. Grass-softened ruts of an old track still led across Dod Moffat's field to it.

Billy walked along slowly, touching each of the posts lightly on its top and whispering its number like a secret code-word. Then he turned and counted back down from sixty-one to one. Some of the posts were rotted at

164

ground level, and hung loose on the fence wires. Posts never rotted above ground, and they never rotted below ground: it was only at ground level they rotted. There was another, still attached. Billy aimed a kick with the sole of his foot: the post flew away from its stump, twanging backwards and forwards and sending a tingling sound all the length of the wires.

High summer. A week into the summer holidays. Two days before, he had been sitting at the Bing when Theresa Thain suddenly appeared out of nowhere, ate some raspberries, remarked that the summer holidays were boring, and went off again. It had shaken Billy. Before Drift had come, the Bing had been his domain; it wasn't a place girls came to. Now Drift had gone, and Theresa Thain had appeared. Somehow she had become intimately related to Drift in Billy's mind. Since the first time he had seen her – that day by the bridge – she had been turning up all over the place. Billy almost admitted to himself now that he actually liked seeing her face, with its clear open grey eyes and fine features, but at the same time it was always with a stab of pain: it was almost as though he felt he would only have to look down, and he would be staring over the parapet of the bridge face to face with that blank-eyed, wild-eyed other stranger who was unaccountably also his own Drift. And now Drift was buried on the land where

Theresa Thain lived.

Billy swung and twanged post twenty-nine and gazed at the white mass that lay over the face of the Tip for a great part of its length. The polystyrene had only been burned at one end before Dod Moffat came rampaging down and insisted that the fire be put out. At that end it was jet-black, fused together in a solid, dead mass, humped and broken like a black moonscape. The rest of the stuff – fissured sheets and blocks and oblongs of it – was white, but it had lost its dazzling whiteness: now it was yellowed, old-looking, like snow in a thaw. Dod Moffat said the rain turned everything brown in the Blackhall area. There had been steady showers for the last two weeks. It was lucky there had been no real wind since March, because the stuff didn't weigh an ounce.

Dod Moffat's old track to the Tip had been churned up in places, as though a heavy vehicle had recently passed along it. Billy frowned. Dod Moffat never used it now. Just across the fence from where the track led, the polystyrene was mounded twice as high as anywhere else.

Seven weeks had passed. They had left a blankness, a dullness, in Billy's mind and emotions, which let him carry on with his everyday life, though he preferred to have something to do. He sometimes wondered vaguely about Geordie Gibbon. He would have liked to have been able to heal the rift he had created, but every time he thought of his friend, the morning of their quarrel returned to his mind – Geordie counting the seconds on his fancy watch; Drift's tongue lolling stupidly; embarrassment at his own childishness – and he couldn't unbend.

If you ran on the polystyrene, it creaked. The big sheets would just take your weight if you ran over them quickly; but quite often there was a pop, and your leg slipped down through. It was hard yet yielding, harmless, yet it could draw blood if it scratched you. It felt warm to your skin on the coldest day. Above all, there was its uncanny lightness.

Billy ran at the high mound of it over from Dod Moffat's track. He did a hurdle-leap onto it, one leg stretched out in front of him. Pop! Crumple. Scratch. A painful scratch. Billy collapsed over onto his side, and drew his leg out to look. It didn't feel like a polystyrene graze. He pulled up the leg of his jeans. Some sharp thing had torn the skin from ankle to knee. Pricks of blood were appearing along the scratch. Billy rolled over to the hole his leg had made. He put his arm into the hole and felt about. There was a sharp edge. A sharp edge to something smooth and cold and – cylindrical. Billy grasped it, and pulled.

The pipe sang as it came out: it must have been lying against a whole lot of others. A

167

whole length of it, twelve, fifteen feet. Three-quarter inch pipe: copper pipe. Billy slid it back in. He pushed his hand into the polystyrene, up to the elbow, up to the armpit. Pipes, stacked in a long, shallow pyramid. He couldn't tell how deep the stack was, but he knew there must be tons of the stuff.

Copper pipe and a tear on his leg. The association was too much. Billy looked around in apprehension. Dave Simmers, Dave Simmers – he could almost hear the name in the rustling of the polystyrene. But there was no one there – no one shouting at him, no one leaping out from a bush to knobble him.

He withdrew. He was suppressing a sudden urge to run. It was like coming on a snake under a stone. Or a rat. He sidled back along the fence, past the strainer, up to the steel fence, along towards the gate of the Yard. He didn't want anyone to see he had been down at the Tip. There was a nameless fear in him, but his mind was turning away, turning away from what he had found. It was shutting out all explanations, the thought of consequences. It was simply telling him, Get out, get out.

He came to the gate, creeping alongside the fence through the broom bushes. He crept through, out onto the road, away.

Trees began. Billy trotted under the striated shadow of the branches arched over the road. The trees marked the edge of the old gardens of Craigmore House. An old stone wall bounded them, mossy, crumbled down. Through them Billy could see the sun bright on the wilderness that had once been the sweeping lawn and shrubbery. Beyond it, the grim blackened west gable of the house itself.

Dod Moffat, his young second wife, their two-year-old son and his wife's nephew lived there now, and that was all. There had been a time when Craigmore House had held thirty people all told, masters and servants. Dod Moffat had been there almost fifty years, since the time he had come up from the Borders and bought both run-down house and farm outright with his father's money. The farm was in good order now, but the house was still a huge, gaunt, dilapidated place, and half its rooms were empty.

Billy crossed through the broken wall, pushed his way in through rhododendron bushes scattering dried petals as he went. Dod Moffat always let him wander there as he wished. "We're all young once," he said, never bothering to explain exactly what he meant. After the rhododendrons there were banks of brambles, but Billy knew a way through. The grass of the old front lawn was long and wet. The dark south face of the house rose at the top of the lawn. Half of it was ivy-grown, but the ivy darkened rather than brightened the look of the house. Only two of the windows on that side belonged to rooms that were used: one was the front room, which was really quite grand but only occupied on special family occasions; the other was Dod's farm office, little more than a cupboard with room for a desk, Dod and a heater. Dod would not be in there just now, but Billy was not sure where he would be at that time of the morning. There were no beasts to feed at this time of year, and milking and clearing up would have been done long since. He wandered down the track to the old steading. It was quiet, with that mournful, deserted look of farm steadings in the summertime before hay and harvest. The two Dutch barns were empty, except for a stairway of straw bales at the end of one of them.

Dod Moffat appeared, walking up the track behind a cow that mooched unhurriedly towards the open gate of a field. She was a black hill-beast, not a milk-cow. She still had her winter coat, rumpled and moth-eaten, half-cast. One of the tits of her udder was huge and swollen, and she held her leg out a little to accommodate it.

Dod shut the gate of the field behind the cow and turned back towards the byres. "It's all full of poison," he remarked over his shoulder to Billy, expecting him to follow.

At the door of the byre a brown calf was lying. It was not much bigger than a large Alsatian, and it was sleek and thin. Its eyes were quite hollow, it must have been dead a couple of days. Billy stopped and looked down into the empty, spectral eyes. They were gazing up into some blackness in the blue sky that no living creature could ever see. Dod Moffat picked up a tube of some cream from the floor of one of the stalls and put it up on a high shelf.

"It was born living," he said, "but there was something wrong with its chest. It's late in the year for calvies anyroad."

"I don't like seeing the dead things," Billy said apologetically.

"I'll need to get it to the knacker," Dod said.

"There's always dead things, isn't there?" Billy said.

"Aye, a good lot," Dod replied, taking off his cap and rubbing his smooth scalp. "There's whiles I think it's downright queer we manage to keep going ourselves for so long." He wheezed and coughed, spat. "You're missing your dog." It was half a remark, half a question.

Billy looked on at the empty eyes of the calf. He nodded.

Dod grunted. "I've a bitch that's had pups today. She's a good working dog, and I was going to sell them. But I can give you one no bother, if you want it." Dod Moffat's normal voice had softened into a bear-like gruffness.

Billy felt a knot gripping his throat. He thought of a puppy, training it, playing with it, getting it to be a proper pet, not a half-wild thing. A black dog, like Dod's. He jumped at it. But on the point of accepting Dod Moffat's offer, the image of the strange golden-eyed thing he had lost sprang into his mind, stronger than at any time in the last seven weeks; its awkward cripple's grace, its warmth and its wisdom. A rush of hot misery into his head made his eyes burn and prickle.

"No thanks, I'd rather not," he heard himself say, a hoarse whisper. He blinked and gritted his teeth and swallowed hard.

"It's all one to me," Dod Moffat said.

Billy knew he had to say something: if he didn't he might start crying, and he couldn't bear to do that in front of the old farmer. Only he couldn't think of anything to say. He racked his brains, desperately, stared at the dead calf and the grey walls of the steading, but his mind was blank. Not even the effort of thinking helped him. Seven weeks of pent-up grief were forcing their way inexorably towards his eyes. The corners of his mouth were pulling themselves down. In a second or two, he would disgrace himself...

Like a last rock in a gathering tide, the pile of copper pipes flashed in on his memory. It was not himself that spoke. It was somebody else inside him using his mouth and speaking instead of him. He listened in wonder as he heard his own voice saying: "I wonder what all the copper pipes are for on the Tip."

It was done. Billy could hardly believe what he had heard. Almost he heard that other person sniggering and turning away, turning back into himself. He caught his breath, waited, staring at the ground.

"What copper pipe's this?" Dod Moffat said. Billy went on looking at the ground. He almost heard the creases on Dod Moffat's forehead gathering into a frown.

"It's – it's just some pipes I found. Somebody must have thrown them out." Billy desperately wondered if sanity had been restored.

It had not. "Your dad wouldn't throw out copper pipes. Copper's getting real valuable. What kind of pipes is it? Are they scrap?" There was unaccustomed urgency in the old voice.

Billy looked up, looked Dod Moffat straight in the eyes. The face was set, each wrinkle tight with alertness, the eyebrows a straight dark bar, the grey eyes diminished in size, hugely increased in intensity. Billy knew what he had done. It was as if he had innocently leaned against a gate and opened it to let out a herd of wild bulls. He had spoken a word to Dod Moffat and set a force of nature on the move. "No," he said, "they're new. It's whole lengths."

"And on the Tip?" Dod Moffat's eyes grew smaller yet.

173

"Under that white stuff."

"Did you not ask your dad?"

"No. I – I forgot." Now it came into Billy's mind that he had betrayed his father.

"Were you feared?"

Billy looked down again. "I suppose."

"How much is there?"

"There's a big pile. I didn't see how much."

"A wagonload?"

"I think so."

"And down on the Tip?" It was half to himself: Dod Moffat was chewing the cud this time.

"Down near the fence."

"Is your dad at the Yard just now?"

"He's working on the compressor."

The force of nature was in motion. "Come on," Dod Moffat said. "I'll need to have a word with him."

DIARY

May 23rd, 1974

I was sitting in the kitchen last night doing
some French when the phone rang. I jumped,
I really did, though I've no idea why. Mum
answered it. I heard her saying, Yes, she's
here; who is it? I was just sitting there
gaping when she came into the kitchen. It's
for you, she said – she sounded really irritated – it's Billy Stuart: I didn't know you
still talked to him. I think, underneath, she
was mad, she was really seething – that's
why she was acting so prim. I don't know
how I got through to the phone. It feels
like I was sitting in the chair one moment
and the next moment I was standing by the
phone.

He said, Hello, Treeza? I said, Hello. I
tried to sound totally cool, but I know my
voice gave me away completely. He didn't
seem to say anything for ages. I wanted to
say something, but I couldn't think of anything to say – my mind was a complete
blank, and I felt so stupid because the way
I'd said hello was such a complete giveaway.
My silence, too. How are you doing? he said.
I said, All right. Another silence. I was getting panicky, because I couldn't think of

anything to say. He said eventually, Can you come over at the weekend? I thought of lots of things, going out with Jemma, what I was going to say to Mum, excuses, all sorts of things. Then I got this sort of overwhelming picture of that ring of red nettles where Drift was buried – actually, I'm not really sure if I did, but I feel *now* as if I did – and my mind went totally quiet. I don't know if I've described that right. I was just going to say "of course" when it was just as if my tongue did a quick flip and the words "what for?" came out instead! I don't know, he said, I'd just like to see you, and I can't come over to your place. Why not? I said. I suddenly felt really angry at the sort of unspoken ban there is on him coming here. Then as soon as I'd said it I froze up because I thought, what if he says OK, I'll come? I'd like to, he said, so I said, really quickly, No, it's OK. Will you come over then? he said, and I said yes.

So we've to meet at two o'clock on Saturday on the old railway track. I felt really cool when I came off the phone, really defiant. I just went and sat down and picked up my book again. Mum said, What did he want? I should have said: permission to visit his dog's grave. But instead I just said he wanted to know about some work. I could see she knew it was a lie, but I didn't even blush.

She said, Doesn't he have anyone else he
can ask? I smiled, oh so sweetly, and said,
I'm the only one in the French class that's
bothering about this exam. Mum turned
away and muttered, I didn't even know he
did French, and I said, Well, he does. I
thought, Well, if she knows so little about me
– and Billy – that she doesn't know I'm not
in the same class as him *for anything* now,
well, that's her fault. Anyway, she's bound to
have heard that we didn't say anything about
French.

I don't know what I'm thinking now. After
Mum had gone away I started trembling like
a jelly, all over. I couldn't even hold my
book.

I'm glad I'm seeing him, though.

May 25th, 1974

Met him. We were together for about a
couple of hours. Spoke about this and that.
Nothing important. Neither of us seemed to
know what to say. We didn't touch. He kept
picking up stones and seeing how far he
could throw them along the track.

I'm just about climbing the wall! But we
agreed to meet again the same place tomorrow.

May 26th, 1974

Typical male! It was pouring with rain. Mum said I was mad going off for a walk in that. I shouted something about it not being half as heavy as she liked to think, and she was just giving me a really queer look when I walked out.

When I say typical male, I mean as soon as we met he put his arms round me and kissed me between the eyes. Between the eyes! It sounds like shooting a dog. "Theresa slumped down in a crumpled heap, pitifully moaning her last." I mean, yesterday it was dry and warm, it was a glorious day, we could have lain in the grass and looked at the clouds, and got really passionate or something – and he spends his time throwing stones; and today, when it's absolutely peeing down and there's no way we can lie down in the grass unless we want a cold bath, he goes and kisses me.

I've just realized that whenever I write about romantic scenes between me and Billy, I start using this really jokey sort of tone. Yet that's not really how I felt about it at all. It must be a defence mechanism.

I don't want to write about everything that happened. I feel too full. I want to keep it all inside myself, not put it down on paper.

A funny thing when I came back, though.

I didn't really think much about it at the time because I was feeling so good, and anyway I was soaking wet.

When I got in Mum was sitting at the kitchen table. She was staring out of the window and she was crying. Of course the first thing I thought – guilt, guilt – was that she knew where I'd been and was upset about it: that she had been angry but now she was heartbroken or something. So I said, What's wrong? She just shook her head and looked a bit grim. So I started to get my wet stuff off – I was a bit amazed she didn't take any notice of the state I was in.

Then I heard her muttering – sort of half to me and half to herself – something about "all those years, and I've never even seen that place of his up on the hill. Stupid old man" – she kept saying that – "stupid, stubborn old man". It was a bit before I realized she must have been talking about Grandad. It's the first time I've seen her getting emotional about him, even mention him – it's almost a year now.

I've never been to his hut either: I used to hear Billy and the other boys talking about it, and I'd think, Hey, he's my grandad, and they all know more about him than I do. Anyway Mum started banging things about in the oven just after that, so we didn't talk about it.

May 30th, 1974

I've been seeing him every day, at lunchtime,
and after school. He's made me tell him some
of what I was getting up to, in April and
that. Some. (I didn't mention Ally Gordon.)
We're going to Bucksburn at the weekend. It
was *my* idea. Since we stopped talking, he
hasn't bothered trying to remember anything.
He said he was too bothered about me.
That's nice, but it worries me a bit too.
Who's really trying to find out about everything – his amnesia, his disappearance, the
accident – him or me? And supposing all
that's really what interests me – *that* and not
him? Well, there's lots of bad things that
could come of that: he could use it to keep
me hanging on, for example. Or something.
Why am I thinking all this? I should just be
feeling happy. I am, I suppose: maybe I'm
worried it's all going to stop. Maybe I'm
pushing this Bucksburn thing so that it does
all stop. Why? Well, things would be all right
with Mum then, wouldn't they? I must stop
this – I'm just trying to depress myself.

June 3rd, 1974

Went to Bucksburn yesterday, then back to
Billy's house afterwards. Billy was really

morose after we got back, and kept going out. His mum was really talkative, though. She was getting ready to go out to her bingo and she was going around in these awful curlers and her slip and she was all slapdash and excited – like Jemma and me when we're going out, but she kept sitting down and talking to me. She told me all about the time when Drift was killed – Billy actually got ill because of it, in bed and delirious and everything. I wish we could have stayed there and spent the evening together too, but we'd arranged to go over to Jemma's and then at the last moment he said he didn't want to go, he wanted to stay by himself and think. I didn't argue too much, because I had this feeling that Something Was Happening – he said he was remembering something, or something, and I thought it was true, I didn't think he was manipulating me. I'm not so sure now, though, because I've just been reading over my last entry here. Anyway, I had to go over and be a gooseberry with Jemma and Roger for the rest of the evening, because I'd told Mum that's where I'd be going. Yeugh. He's all right, I suppose, but how can she go out with someone called Roger?

Anyway – I'm starting at the wrong end. We went in on the bus yesterday afternoon. Billy and me, I mean. It really feels like every-

thing was just there waiting for us. We went
right through the town on the bus again
and got off at that industrial estate. It's
funny, it seemed quite a pleasant, warm day,
but as soon as we got in among those big
blank buildings it was like being in a different climate. They tower over you, all grey
and expressionless. So desolate.

Anyway, that's just Treeza being impres-
sionable. I saw the signboard this time. It
said MAXWELL'S LAYERS. It wouldn't have
made any sense to me, but there were two
hens and a cock, just silhouettes, at opposite
ends of the board. So it was a chicken factory.
Just before we got to it (we were just walking
up the pavement, and I'd slipped my arm
into his and was feeling up and down the
inside of his arm – I like doing that), when I
suddenly felt him stiffen. I mean, he went
really hard, all over. His *body*, I mean – oh
God, the way my mind works. His *muscles*
tightened, and he stopped. There was a man
walking down towards us, from the place
that said Maxwell's Layers. He didn't look
like anything special, didn't look bad – or
good – or anything, he had curly hair and he
was wearing pale blue overalls. I said, What
is it? He glanced at me – I mean, Billy did –
but his jaw was set in a queer way, I'd never
seen him looking like that before, and I got
this stupid momentary thought: he's forgot-

ten how to speak. Then suddenly he said,
Across here – and next thing he was dragging
me off running across the road, then back
down towards the town, and up some other
road and I don't know where else, running
like crazy. I think I was screaming something
at him but he didn't take any notice, and I
kept running, hanging on to him. He didn't
stop until we were out of the industrial estate
and then we sat down on some grass and we
were both gasping for breath for ages. I was
really panicked but I couldn't say anything to
him until I'd got my breath back. Then I
thought he was going to be sick. He looked
like dough and he was bending over as if he
was trying to throw up. I kept saying, What
is it? What's wrong? and eventually he said,
That man. I said, What about him? And he
bent over and heaved a bit more and then he
said, It was Dave Simmers.

Well, all I'd seen was the curly hair but
apart from that it certainly didn't look to me
like Dave Simmers – not how I remembered
him anyway. But all I said was, It was *not*. I
was just trying to soothe him, but he kept
shaking his head, and then he blurted out
something like, I've seen it – like that –
before – just like him. Something like that,
really incoherent, and he kept shaking his
head and rubbing his face with his hands and
making his hair all tangled. Then he said,

Come on, and jumped up, and we went back
into the town. I was waiting for him to say
something else about it – I didn't really want
to ask him any more – but he didn't, and
after a bit he became quite normal again.

June 5th, 1974

(Still continuing – I didn't have time to write
last night.) The rest of the day was really
nice. We ate ice-cream, and held hands, wandered about, looked at shops. I made Billy
look at all the engagement rings in the jew-
eller's window. I think he was getting really
jumpy! I said, I'd want a *boy* first, and he
kind of curled up and shoved his hands into
his pockets and muttered.

There's this really posh woman we see in
church, and we met her in the main street!
Oh God, I thought, this is it. She was wearing a turquoise green hat with a pin stuck in
it. She's always wearing a hat, even in the
warmest weather. I just about dropped dead
when she gave me this huge great beaming
smile and said hello – really nicely, really
genuine. Billy said, Who's that old cow? I
said she comes to church. He said, That's just
the kind of folk that goes to church, that's
why I'll never go – like Geordie's mam was.
It was funny. Funny about Geordie's mum,

too. In a way, I think Billy's really relieved Geordie's gone away – it's like he doesn't have to *bother* about all that friendship stuff any more.

When we were in the bus on the way home he suddenly said, See that place? It's full of hens cooped up in wee cages. They lay their eggs on a wire thing, and it rolls down a wee chute into a wee basket. The light's on all the time, and there's no windows. Dad got twelve hens from there once, and three of them died because they couldn't stand the fresh air. There's still eight of them now, they run with Dod Moffat's birds. So you know that place? I said. I didn't, but I do now, he said. Then a bit later he said, It wasn't Dave Simmers we saw, it was his brother: he works there. After a minute or two he started laughing. It was a bit freaky, the way he just started laughing, quite quietly, to himself. I said, What is it? – a bit panicky, I didn't like the way he was laughing, I began to think I was sitting next to a maniac. He stopped laughing but the next thing he said was more to himself than to me, something about white birds going up into the trees, and he said that with a bit of a laugh, as if he'd just seen through a joke, or a riddle. I remember now he said something about white birds before, to do with the accident. I thought I'd written it down earlier, but I can't find it now. He didn't speak much after that, and he seemed to be thinking hard. I asked him, Are you starting to remember something? and he nodded.

June 10th, 1974

I think there's still something going on under the surface with Billy, but he's all right in other ways. We haven't been talking about It. I don't like to pester him, and I just like to be with him normally, while I still can. I wonder what I mean by that?

June 13th, 1974

It's funny how things change. Perhaps I will get closer to them again – Dad anyway. It's over five months since that really good conversation I had with him, in the Christmas holidays, and then I had that dream and everything seemed to get bad again. It's time they changed again.

I was coming back from school today. I always get the school bus to stop at the wood now, not at the road-end. The driver used to make a fuss about that sort of thing, but I just flutter my eyelashes at him now and he does what I ask. Power! Anyway, I always like going back through the wood. Drift's wood. Driftwood. I like to think of how it was six months ago, when I used to have those dreams about Billy coming along that track and I got so scared. Now all that seems to be on the other side of somewhere – the other side of a hill, "down under" in deepest Tasmania, on the dark side of the moon...

I've just realized why I mentioned Tasmania. It was because of a song Mr Arnott played us in English when we were studying Scottish ballads and that. It was really beautiful and I'm always humming it over. It starts:

No lark in transport mounts the sky
Or leaves with early plaintive cry
But I must bid a last goodbye
A last fareweel to Stirling, O.

Though far awa', my heart's with you
Our youthful hours upon wings they flew
But I must bid a last adieu,
A last fareweel to Stirling, O.

He's being deported for poaching, and he's saying goodbye to his girl and that (he leaves her his gun and his dog – that bit really gets me), and his punishment's to be sent to do hard labour in Tasmania for twenty years. *Twenty years!* My God, I thought about when he came back, and he'd be quite old, and she'd have got married and got a family and everything – it was awful. They call Tasmania "Van Dieman's Land" – that makes it sound worse somehow: I think of demons and things.

Anyway, I'm being scatterbrained. I was coming through the wood yesterday when I met Dad. He was sorting the fence. He asked me if I'd forgotten which was my stop – something like that. Joking. I said, no, I just like walking through the wood. Why's that now, he said, do you like getting your knees tickled by the nettles – or do those nylon things protect you from everything natural? He's so different when he's outside. I almost felt as if I was being chatted up, it was very strange. I didn't quite know what to say. But I was feeling so sort of warm and friendly – and honest, I just came out with it and told him I liked going there because that was where Drift was buried. What's Drift? he said. I said, That was Billy Stuart's dog. Oh aye, he said. He was hammering staples in, so it was: *Bang, bang, bang.* Pause. "Oh aye." *Bang, bang, bang.* Then he stopped banging, and seemed to be thinking. So I popped the question: Can you show me the exact place you buried him, please? He looked round at me, so I thought it was worth smiling and fluttering my eyelashes a bit. He looked away and fished some more

staples out of his pocket. I thought he was
going to start hammering again, but then he
stopped and rested the hammer head on one
of the fence wires and stood looking down at
his boots. Oh, he said, I don't just know if
I'd remember the exact spot any more, it
must be two years since it happened. I
reminded him it was just last year, and he
said "Oh well, then" and sort of scratched
his head and peered off towards the wood.
It's amazing how little difference a year
makes to him.

He took me straight to the place, of
course. It wasn't the bit I'd thought: it was a
bit I'd never even noticed, a little humped
mound. There weren't any nettles growing
on it, just little thin weeds, that's why I'd
never noticed it. We just stood and looked at
it. What else can you do.

Dad said, His dad's doing well, it's a different place up there now. I didn't say anything – I had this feeling Dad was trying to
get something out of me about Billy. And he
went on – I always thought Will Stuart
would come to grief if he took up with that
Andy Gibbon, but I'm glad everything's
sorted itself out now. I was still determined
not to give anything away, and I asked him,
quite suddenly, Did you shoot him? I meant
Drift, of course. He said, No! with a short
kind of laugh. You couldn't disbelieve him.

It's a bad bit of the road, that, he said, what with the bend and then the wood – well, we should know that. I suppose he was talking about the Accident. He said it would be quite easy for Drift to have been killed by a car and never had a mark on him. Poor Drift: to survive getting run over by a tractor, just to get killed by a car six months later.

As we were going back, he suddenly said, I was talking with Edwina McLeod the other day in Blackhall. Who's that? I said, though I guessed straight away. He said, It's that old body that lived in India for years, we see her at the Kirk, she's a fine old bird. He got to where his hammer was and picked it up and just sort of remarked over his shoulder, She was saying she'd met you in Bucksburn. He fished his staples out again. He never looked at me. I just said, Oh; and he started hammering. I just stood rooted to the spot. Eventually he said, Tell your mother I'll be in late for my tea, I want to get this stretch finished. And I said, OK, and went on my way.

There's no one else it could have been: it must have been the Hat Woman. But I'm sure if he'd told Mum she'd have said something to me. I'm also sure that old Edwina would have said that she saw Theresa *and her boyfriend* – not nastily, she just wouldn't have known what Mum was like. And Dad told me to let me know that he *knew*.

What I mean is, Dad must be on my side. But maybe he wants me to tell them what I'm up to.

I want to, but I don't know if I can.

June 17th, 1974

(Continuing) I don't even know if I know myself. Sometimes I even think it's not Billy I want at all, but just his secret. The secret of what happened that night, of the white birds – of his disappearance.

Package 9

Hobart
August 8, 1984

Dear Roger,

I'm sorry, I'm sorry, I'm sorry. It was
ten years ago, I was young and foolish,
now I'm sadder and wiser. All right?
Now the name "Roger" means for me all
that is steady, reliable, loyal, sensi-
tive, handsome, sexy – need I go on?
You know you're the only friend from
schooldays that I still keep in touch
with. Besides, I was just jealous of
Jemma. At the exalted age of seventeen,
you really were such a man of the
world, or so it seemed to us then.

About the other business – I'll take
it as being a comment on *me*, not on the
story, so I shall go on sending you
chapters – but beware! Anyway, I'm not
going to make any apology. OK, I wan-
gled my way into Billy Stuart's affec-
tions because he was feeling vulnerable
after losing his dog. What of it?
That's nature's way. Let me tell you
that new people don't get born into

this world as a result of wonderful friendships between boys and dogs, if you get my drift (sorry, that was bad). I was a force of nature. I was "only doing what I was supposed to do."

As you see, I've been hammering on with the Story (this was supposed to have been two chapters, but I've run them into one) - so no diary this time.

A.E.

T.T.

CHAPTER
8

PETER WARD

Billy and Dod Moffat came out of the cool shadows of the byre into the sunlight. They made their way downhill, through and past the last corner of the old steading building. The old farmer muttered and wheezed, as if carrying on an ancient conversation with someone Billy couldn't see. The warm sun of the last few days had baked the mud hard, but here and there the black polished top of a cobblestone was humped up through the rough dun surface.

They passed a dog chained at the corner. Billy held out his hand to it, but the dog cringed back against the wall. "I wouldn't trust that one," Dod muttered. "It'll take your fingers off."

They went on. "You can never trust a dog that's tied up," Dod said. "He's not feared at you, see, he's feared at himself. He'd attack his

194

own shadow."

Below the steading was a wasteland, a dump for several decades of accumulated farm stuff, stuff put aside, perhaps for use "later", and then forgotten about. Nettles grew everywhere, already waist-high, all but covering the crazy loops and nets of rusty fence wire, completely obliterating everything else apart from the handles of an old horse plough. These could still be seen, eaten away with rust, pointing up at the sky as if long ago the plough had inexplicably nosedived out of the clouds into the soft black soil. A narrow path wound through the nettles and the great tangles of wire, and Dod Moffat led Billy down it, muttering something about needing to get the place tidied up one of these days.

They crossed a ditch and a belt of larch trees, and began to climb the pasture back up towards the Yard.

Dod Moffat aimed for the Tip, and they climbed up over the burnt polystyrene, where the ground was covered in the hard, crinkled black mass. Some of it crunched as they walked on it, some of it was quite hard. "It'll be a while before anything grows here," Dod Moffat remarked. Billy wondered if he was angry, but his face was as expressionless as a rock. He had merely been stating a fact. Muttering and wheezing still, Dod climbed up through the Tip, and Billy followed him, wondering anxiously what he was going to say to his father. He felt like slipping away and taking cover in one of the old hulks of vehicles that here and there stood reared up at odd angles; but something else, not courage, made him hold his ground hard at the farmer's heels.

Will Stuart gave the smallest start of surprise when he saw the pair of them coming towards him, threading their way through the broom bushes from the Tip. They made a grotesque pair, even a little sinister: the great hulk of the farmer with his lumbering gait next to the lithe light-stepping boy, emerging from nowhere. Will Stuart straightened up. "What's ado?" he said.

"Nothing, nothing at all," Dod Moffat said dismissively. "It's a rare fine day."

"Grand," Will Stuart said; and waited, silent. He was standing, his hands black to the wrists, beside a battered yellow compressor, a heavy hammer balanced loosely across his curled fingers.

"It's a while," Dod Moffat said, "since we were up to see Peter Ward." He turned back from a brief contemplation of the clouds to glance at Will Stuart.

"It is, aye." Another silence. Billy started tracing a copy of the compressor's radiator grille in a dusty hollow where a puddle had been, criss-crossing the lines as meticulously as he could with the side of his sandshoe.

Dod Moffat turned away and began his contemplation of the sky again.

"Ach, all right," Will Stuart said suddenly, throwing his hammer onto the top of the compressor, where it clanked and sent flakes of yellow paint showering off. He bent down, picked a cloth up from his toolkit and wiped his hands. It was a gesture, mainly: it made little difference to the state of them. He pulled his jacket off the compressor's exhaust pipe and said, "I'll go and tell the lads – just you carry on."

The three of them crossed from the gate of the Yard, squeezed through the fence and began their uphill trek through the rough grass and heather towards the distant shimmer of green that was the Moss wood. Billy could not think what Dod Moffat was up to, but he supposed it was all part of a carefully worked-out plan – like the detour they had made in order to be seen casually coming into the Yard from the direction of the Tip. He felt immense relief and gratitude at the old man's sensitivity, and knew he could rely on him not to put over the impression that Billy had rushed over to Dod Moffat to tell him about the pipes.

The day was very warm, and the warmth increased on the unsheltered hill. The heather threw back the heat at them. The sweat was pouring off Dod Moffat's forehead, and he swore. "I don't think I can keep up with you young lads," he said. They stopped, grinning, and looked back on the path they had come. The world seemed to have been reduced to a bright picture of green emerald and blue amethyst. Whin-bushes grew about them, here and there a rowan or a birch tree, and the faint apricot scent of a few late whins hung around. Two larks were singing, high up, out of sight in the dazzling air, but otherwise there was silence; not a breeze stirring.

"Away on up," Dod said to Billy, "and catch us a couple of coneys." He winked at Will Stuart. Billy grinned, and trotted off up towards the Moss. He dived off among the whins, leaving the path, making for the right-hand side of the wood where the trees dipped down out of sight behind the line of the hill.

It was not until he was well out of sight of the two men that he stopped. He had no wish to catch rabbits. That belonged to the time before Drift, and everything was different now. Dod Moffat wasn't concerned about whether he caught rabbits either, of course: he had simply wanted Billy out of the way. Billy continued on towards the Moss: he would go there, but not as he used to, back in what seemed to be another lifetime.

He dawdled. He kicked up the dry whin-needles when he crossed them; he stripped the fresh sprigs of broom from their thin branches when he passed them; he skirted the lower side of the Moss, sat on a tussock, and stared moodily at the broad valley of the Forth spreading in the blue distance, the haze of smoke over Falkirk and the etched black line of the Stirling hills. His mood became dreamy and vague, and after a while he started, and wondered if he had been asleep. He felt as if he had been on the verge of stepping over into something else, or somewhere...

He shook his head. What was it? A feeling almost as if things were going on, right next to him, under him, around him, but that he couldn't see: that no one could ever see, and that most of the time, on ordinary days, you weren't in the least aware of. Billy didn't care for it. He jumped to his feet and ran uphill into the wood, trying to leave the strange sensation behind, trying to outrun it. After a while normality seemed to return and he stopped running. He went softly between the birch trees and the tussocks of wiry grass.

At the peat bank he stopped. The surface of the peat was beginning to dry. It looked like chocolate, and Billy felt hungry. Gradually he became aware of voices. He knew it would be Dod Moffat and his father, and stood still, not wishing to interrupt them. But he found himself straining his ears to listen. He could hear the voices, and recognized well enough who they belonged to, but couldn't make out the words. At length he dropped to his hands and knees, crawled some way forward from the peat bank, then stretched himself flat, as softly as if he had been going to wait for rabbits, and peered forward through the trees. Now he could see Dod Moffat's flat grey cap and his father's curly brown hair just over a ridge of grass, where they sat half-facing each other, each with his back to a tree. Their voices were clear in the hill-silence, but there was something about his father's voice which Billy did not recognize: a wheedling tone was in it, almost a whine, which Billy found entirely new. He seemed to be trying to explain something.

"Look at Andy, now," he was saying. "He's got his own house – ach, and a mortgage right enough, but the house is his own. It's the *standards*, do you understand, that he's letting his family have. Take holidays now. Me, I've never been out of Scotland in my life. I've never been further than Dunoon. And nor's my family. But see Andy? He's off to Spain – Austria – Greece. He's offering more to his bairns. Travel broadens the mind, it's right enough. You should see the hi-fi equipment he's got, tape recorders, I don't know what. A freezer twice the size of an old meal-kist. Right enough, his wife's getting a good wage too. I don't have that sort of things to offer young Billy there. He'll grow up just like me: ignorant. Aye, I dare say it's Mrs Gibbon that's given him all these ideas in the first place, but you see, he's accepted—"

"Come on, man!" Dod Moffat burst in, his voice rising high and hoarse as it did when he was excited or angry. Billy crept forward, inch by inch, through the grass until he could see the faces of the two men as well as the tops of their heads. Dod Moffat's face was flushed and angry. "Come on," he was saying, "my wife was a teacher just the same as Andy's. I'm not pretending we got on – that's not what I'm saying – but she never tried to influence me with any fancy ideas. Christ, a farmer's wife was what she was and she knew well enough what the story was. But Christ, man" – Billy could see Dod pounding the turf with his fist – "what are you wanting out of life? Continental holidays? And what does Andy get out of them but some foreign bug on his gut that keeps him on the toilet for two nights at a stretch? Pull yourself together, man – what more have you ever wanted than to have enough money to pay your rent and have a drink with your pals and keep the taxman away from the door? You know that fine, and so do I."

A heavy silence fell between the two of them. Billy could see Dod Moffat's rock-like face working as he clenched and unclenched his jaws, his mouth almost disappearing between puckered top lip and puckered chin.

201

Will Stuart's face was blank, expressionless, his head sunk forward, deep in gloom.

Billy backed off silently, onto the peat bank and out of sight. When he felt low enough down, he stood up and leaped noisily back up to the top of the bank. Both men looked up as he approached.

"Well, Billy," Dod Moffat said, "your dad and I are just having a quiet wee conversation here. How are you doing? Have you not caught us anything?"

"No," Billy said. He stood uncertainly, while his hand found the trunk of a small birch tree and began automatically stripping off the paper-like bark. He looked at Dod Moffat's feet, and then his father's feet, but he couldn't look them full in the face. He realized neither of them was going to move, and neither was going to continue the conversation while he was there. Everything seemed fixed. "Can I go on up?" he asked suddenly.

His father grunted, nodded. Billy didn't waste time. Everything seemed so strange and still, the two men the worst of the lot, as still as stones sitting in the grass. He would risk Peter Ward on his own. He took to his heels, up the path, up the hill, out of the Moss, where everything was so quiet and not even a bird sang.

He ran until he was out of breath and the hair on his forehead was plastered with sweat.

He turned and looked round. The land had fallen away behind him. The Moss was a haze of vibrant green among the other greens of the moor, heather-green, grass-green, whin-green. Visible now but very distant, Davieburn was a dulling of the air, a slight smokiness among the farmlands criss-crossed by their belts of trees. Billy turned on uphill again; he was nearing the top of the path. A sheep's skull stared up at him, half-buried in the grass, half-hidden under a whin-bush. The tops of the trees around Peter Ward's hut came into sight over the brow of the hill, disappearing and reappearing as the path went through dips and hollows.

Then the ridge of ground in front of him crawled down off the trees, until Billy could see all of the hut in its dark little hollow. He stopped. No smoke was coming out of the stovepipe, but the door stood wide open.

Billy paused, thinking of the conversation in the Moss. Now that he saw Peter Ward's hut, he felt a little shy of going down by himself. But he didn't know how much longer Dod Moffat and his father would be. His head was whirling a little with the thought of continental holidays and freezers and hi-fi equipment. None of these things were of any great interest to him, and the whirl of thoughts always seemed to come back and crystallize into that image of the two stones sitting in the grass of

203

the Moss and conversing in the incomprehensible silent language of stones. He knew Dod Moffat was trying to help. Somehow, implicitly, he knew it and trusted him; but he could not get his mind around the question of what exactly the old farmer was trying to do.

He took a few steps forward, then stiffened. There was something following. He heard nothing, but he was sure. Not the heavy steps of Dod Moffat and his father toiling up the path, but something other, something that went along without a sound on the short grass. Slowly, grudgingly, Billy willed himself to turn round.

There was nothing. The day was as bright as ever, basking in its early afternoon haze. There was not a sign of living thing anywhere near. Billy stared at the path dwindling down behind him, at its stones, at the stunted whin-bushes. Gradually he began to relax. A lark left the ground not twenty yards away from him, climbing on its giant steps up into the clear air, bubbling and glittering with song. Billy frowned. He turned back towards Peter Ward's hut. Why was it so dark down there? The trees around it, tall shapely ash-trees, cast only a light shade, and yet it seemed almost dusk down in the hollow, as if evening were already falling.

Stolen copper. Billy had not used the word "stolen" yet, even to himself; but it must have been there, under the threshold of his mind, all along. He had grown up in a world where risky deals were part of everyday life. Not to the disadvantage of neighbours, of course, and certainly not of friends. With people like Mr Venay, the owner of the Bridge, it was a slightly different matter: he cheated anyone he could, being an outsider and ill-at-ease, so he was fair game if, say, a few bottles of whisky were left lying around. Nobody looked on that as *stealing*, exactly. And then again, if half a dozen brand-new tyres or a drum of tractor oil should happen to come along, and the man who brought them was a bit hazy about their origins or why he was selling them so cheaply, no questions were asked: the items were simply got rid of again, at a small profit, as quickly as possible. With that sort of deal, ordinary small folk were getting a little of their own back at "them", the big, the powerful, the *others*. But a lorry load – or more – of new copper was a different matter.

Billy couldn't put a value on it, but he knew it was worth a lot. What was more, he knew it was tied up with Dave Simmers in some way. He also knew that his father had little to do with Dave Simmers, so the connection must run through Andy Gibbon – Andy Gibbon who had continental holidays, and hi-fi equipment, and a BMW. But then his father had looked like a naughty boy caught in the act,

205

that evening when he watched Dave Simmers come up to the Yard – so his father must be involved in some way.

Or was Andy Gibbon trying to persuade him to become involved? Was that what that scene had really been about, that day – that same day when he had come eye to eye with Drift the stranger, and Theresa Thain the stranger, at the railway bridge, and Dod Moffat and Dave Simmers had come to blows? It all seemed to fall into place. Andy Gibbon was trying to persuade his father to come in on the arrangement with the copper, and Dave Simmers was egging Andy Gibbon on. Dave Simmers arranged things: he had an arrangement with his brother about the hens at the chicken factory; he had an arrangement with Andy Gibbon over the copper. The more people he had involved in his arrangements, the safer he felt – the more in control.

Billy blamed Dave Simmers for Drift's death: it was the kick to the head which had started the dog running away. His fear of Simmers, whom he thought of as little as possible, had become mixed with a deep, rugged loathing. Dod Moffat, on the other hand, stood in his mind against this emissary of evil. But now, for once, he saw things reversed. Who, for instance, was to say that Dod Moffat was right? He had a big house and a big farm: he might look like a tramp, but that was only because he chose to look that way. Billy had heard his father say that numerous times. Peter Ward too. It was fine acting poor if you were really rich. And if he, Billy, had a fiver a week in pocket money, what might he not get with it? Not a fancy watch, maybe, but a decent bike, anyway, for a kick-off...

Like a blow in the back, that other feeling struck him again. There *was* something behind him! He swung round, sweat prickling his skin. Again he saw nothing. But now a shadow was imprinted on his mind, as if something had been there: not something of man-height, but something that went low to the ground. Something just at the edge of his mind's vision, that he could almost put a shape, put a name, to, if only he could shift his vision a little to the side...

At that moment there was a rattle and a squeak, and looking back to the hut Billy saw Peter Ward coming round the side of it with a barrowful of chopped sticks. He looked up immediately and saw Billy, put the barrow handles down and waited. Billy went down towards him.

He found the shadow under the trees downright queer. He kept glancing up, but the sky was as blue as ever.

"Well, you're on your own today?" Peter Ward said. Billy was never sure if Peter Ward actually remembered him, and it was impossible to tell from this greeting.

"My dad's just coming," he said. Then, almost despite himself, he added: "It's awful dark here." He had never before dared to initiate conversation with Peter Ward.

"You don't get proper sunshine here any more," Peter Ward replied, as if confirming an obvious statement.

"What do you mean?" Again, Billy was startled at the strangeness of it: he had always been tongue-tied before.

"Come in – come in, lad," said Peter Ward. "Oh – you can help me with my sticks first. I've been getting going on the big tree I took down last summer."

But then, he had never been alone with Peter Ward before. "I never heard a saw," he said, thinking of the big silence on the way up the hill.

"No," the old man said enigmatically.

Billy let him pile the wood into his arms, then carried it into the hut and stacked it in the stone hearth around the stove. He made two trips with an armful of the sticks, and then Peter Ward followed him in with the remainder. They knelt, side by side, at the hearth, stacking their sticks in silence. Billy, for the first time in that hut, felt wholly at ease.

"What do you mean about the sunshine?" he asked again.

Peter Ward rose slowly to his knees, and

went over to the untidy bed. He sat on it, resting his back against the wall, laid his hands palms up in his lap, and sighed. He looked tired, but the eyes resting on Billy were sharp.

"What I mean, William," he said, "is that what's gone is gone. When did you last pick brambles?"

"Brambles?" Billy was taken aback.

"Have you ever picked brambles?"

"Aye, of course," Billy said.

"No, I'm not meaning like that," Peter Ward said impatiently. "Not the odd one or two to your hand on the way back from school. I mean really picking them – going out for a whole day picking them, and then coming back at teatime with great baskets full of them, aye, and not these tatty wee things you get now, but great juicy things as big as the end of my thumb. Enough for pies, and a shelfful of jam, and wine too – they make a rare red wine. That's what we got when I was a boy."

"I've never done that," said Billy.

"That ash tree I took down there," Peter Ward went on. "It wasn't full-grown, but it was done. Finished. It was withered at the ends of its branches. The leaves stopped, like, about that much from the end" – he spread out thumb and little finger of one hand – "and then there was just the bare twigs all round the edges of it."

209

Billy waited, trying to follow the gist of the old man's tirade. He understood only that he was speaking from passionate conviction.

"That's what it is, you see," Peter Ward said. "It's all poisoned now. The air's poisoned."

That was the kind of thing Dod Moffat said. Billy was disappointed. It was the kind of meaningless thing the old people were always saying. It said nothing about the strangely darkening air here.

"You lost your dog, I hear," Peter Ward said suddenly.

At last Billy was tongue-tied. He stiffened, down on his knees in front of the hearth, and kept his eyes fixed on the pile of firewood. He felt the hawk-like gaze of the old man boring into the side of his head. How did Peter Ward know about Drift, if his father and Dod Moffat hadn't been up to see him lately?

"What was his name?" The voice was gentle.

"Drift."

"It's an ill thing, losing a dog."

The split ash-wood was milky white. Faint lark-song bubbled in from the open doorway.

"Now," Peter Ward said, "I've got a job for you. Take the wheelbarrow round the back and get another load of wood to me. Since you're here, I may as well act my age." He rose to his feet and went, a little stiffly, to the table in the middle of the floor. Billy did as he was told.

It seemed bright at first outside, after being in the hut. Billy looked around for a moment, but saw nothing moving. He turned the barrow, and squeaked to the first corner of the hut. There, the air darkened again perceptibly. It was like stirring up a light sediment in a glass of water: not enough to stop it being transparent, but enough to cast a murk through it. And the air seemed to be thicker, too. At first Billy thought it must be the ill-oiled wheelbarrow, and pushed harder, leaning forward over the handles. But soon he felt he was actually pushing through heavy air that was swathed round him. The way down the long side of the hut seemed endless. And yet there was still not a cloud in the sky.

Three steps more, Billy thought. Two. One. He reached the second corner of the hut. Then stopped dead.

The landscape had changed completely.

"I'm putting myself on the line here," Dod Moffat growled. "I hope you'll not let me down."

"Never fear, Dod," said Will Stuart. "I've made my mind up."

"Mr Gibbon's got a persuasive tongue."

"I've made my mind up, Dod," Will Stuart repeated, with quiet emphasis. "As soon as we get down today, I'll have a look at that bit of ground. It'd be fine to be working on my own, I can't deny – but you're a crafty old devil: you'd never have gotten round to clearing that mess yourself."

Dod Moffat grunted. They were looking down at Peter Ward's hut in its hollow under the trees. The day was as bright and lovely as ever, the lark singing high above the ridge they were standing on. "Fair enough," he said, and sniffed; and then, with the twinkle of mischief that occasionally cracked the rock-like casing, "Why, man, you're looking ten years younger already – we'll need to do a deal like this every week."

They walked down the track together to the wooden hut.

Through the open door they saw Peter Ward sitting at his table. He was very upright, motionless, his hands resting on the bare wooden surface in front of him. He seemed to be gazing distantly through the small window.

"You alone, Peter?" Dod Moffat said.

Peter Ward turned his head. He was looking towards them but seemed not entirely aware of them. But he spoke affably enough. "Come in, aye, come in," he said. "I'm getting a rare crowd of visitors today. The good weather brings you out like flies."

They crowded into the hut. Peter Ward looked at them steadily, but there was a dimness in his eyes. He looked like a man not well or in pain, though it was hard to tell, coming into the gloom of the hut from the bright day.

"Are you well, Peter?" Will Stuart said.

"I'm well enough, thank you, Will," he answered, "but I'm not getting any younger." He grinned at Dod Moffat. "Nor are you, Dod, I see. Why, man, you're sweating like a pig."

Dod Moffat took off his cap and wiped his forehead. "Age, and overmuch good living," he said.

"A young wife, Peter, you see," Will Stuart put in. "It takes it out of an old man."

"There's a bottle," Peter Ward said, "on the top shelf of the cupboard. And some glasses. You'll get them, Will, will you?"

The amber liquid glowed in the three glasses. The bottle was a gallon bottle of whisky – a donation, indirectly, from the Bridge Bar.

They toasted, and drank.

"Has Billy been in to see you?" Will Stuart asked.

"He was in by half an hour ago, yes," Peter Ward answered. "I sent him round to get a barrow of wood."

"He brought it, did he?"

"No," Peter Ward said, "he's not come back yet."

"Little devil," said Will Stuart.

"Ach, leave him be. He's all right. He's got a long way to go." Again the old man gazed away. "At that age," he said, "you've got to give them their freedom."

Will Stuart was pacified, and they finished their whisky in silence.

"Have you been cutting sticks?" Dod Moffat asked.

"The big ash tree," Peter Ward said. "The one I took down."

"How bad was it?"

"Bad enough. But it'll keep me warm for a while!"

They talked, musing on the big ash and other trees of their acquaintance. Then Dod Moffat got up, saying he was going to have a look at it. Will Stuart went with him. Peter Ward excused himself and remained sitting at the table, just as before. "I've seen enough of it for one day," he smiled, and turned again to the window.

The two men went round the side of the hut just as Billy had done before, strolling, hands in their pockets. Relief and the whisky had greatly mellowed Will Stuart's mood: he looked at one with the world.

At the corner of the hut they came on the wheelbarrow, empty. "He's not even filled it," Will Stuart muttered.

The big ash tree was felled across the slope.

Silver-grey, stone-like, it looked even larger than it had done when standing. Its branches had been lopped off, and lay scattered around. A ghost-growth of stunted leaves made a green haze of the branch-ends. An axe was buried in one large branch, the handle pointing up the hill towards the hut.

Dod Moffat frowned. "Not like Peter to leave his tools lying about when he's finished."

"I wonder where that Billy's gone," Will Stuart said.

"He'll be around."

"Somewhere in the blue beyond." Will Stuart shrugged. There was a small, secret wood of hawthorns in the little valley down which Peter Ward's spring flowed. The blossoms were gone, but the dusky-gleaming leaves and the thin black trunks stood out dreamily among the lush grass.

They examined the trunk of the ash tree, leisurely noting the extent of the rottenness at its heart, and then turned back towards the hut. Will Stuart filled the barrow up with chopped sticks, and trundled it back up the side of the hut and round to the door.

"You want the wood inside, Peter?" Dod Moffat called.

Peter Ward was sitting exactly as they had left him, exactly as they had first seen him, hands resting on the table, eyes fixed on the little window. He did not answer.

215

"Eh, Peter?" Dod Moffat called again. Still there was no answer.

The two men exchanged a quick, puzzled, glance. "What's up now?" Dod muttered, climbing the steps into the hut. Will Stuart followed him in. Peter Ward remained motionless.

"Peter? Peter? Are you all right? Christ," Dod Moffat said, turning to Will Stuart, "take a look at this now."

Peter Ward was dead.

It was a long afternoon. Back at Craigmore farm, they phoned for the doctor. Dod Moffat cranked up his ancient Land Rover, and went with him round by the road and up the stony track, with Will Stuart and the two boys from the Yard bouncing on a pile of blankets behind. Andy Gibbon was away in Edinburgh, so the Yard had to be locked up behind them.

The doctor pronounced Peter Ward dead of a heart attack, but the police had to be called all the same. Peter Ward's brother had to be phoned up so that Peter's wife could be informed.

By the time they were all quite finished, and Peter Ward's body driven off, it was well past seven o'clock. They congregated in the Bridge.

The main talk that evening was of Peter

Ward, and there was much recounting of the rumour and legends, and true tales as well, that had grown up around the old eccentric's name.

In a way, that played into Dod Moffat's hands. He had kept his head clear through all the shock and excitement, and was more anxious for the living than for the dead. Andy Gibbon was a persuasive man; but on the other hand a decision well discussed around the neighbourhood was a decision taken for granted in the neighbourhood, and Dod Moffat wanted the neighbourhood firmly behind Will Stuart's decision as soon as possible. Everyone was taken up with Peter Ward, Andy Gibbon was not yet returned to draw attention to the business, so Dod Moffat had little difficulty in slipping it into the conversation with all the best gossips and rumour mongers: Will Stuart had decided to break up his partnership with Andy Gibbon, and was getting the lease of a smaller area of ground just below the steading at Craigmore for a new Yard. As the more popular man, Will could expect to corner the more local market, while Andy Gibbon, if he wished, could spread himself farther afield.

Dod was glad he had made the effort. The rumour generated its own momentum, and Will Stuart's decision was ratified by common consent even though his mind was soon taken up with a far more immediately pressing problem.

It was very late before Will Stuart got home that night. He was annoyed with himself, because he wanted to have the chance to tell his wife about the new agreement, and explain his reasons, tell her something of the increasingly risky deals Andy Gibbon was dragging the Yard into. Now she was certain to have gone to bed and he would have to wait until tomorrow. He was not drunk, although he was not entirely sober either.

All the lights in the house were on when he arrived back. That was strange: it was after midnight. Even stranger, Beth Stuart was not only still up, but still dressed. She was sitting at the table in the kitchen, her hands in her lap, her eyes dark-rimmed in her pale, blank face. She glanced past him as he came in, but in a half-resigned way, as if she had been looking for someone else but knew no one else was there.

"What's up, Beth?" Will Stuart asked uncertainly. She was not angry, but she was definitely upset.

She stared at him blankly. "He's not with you."

"Who?"

"Billy."

"No. Why? Have you not—"

"He's never been back since he left with you

this morning. Oh, Will, there's something wrong, I know there is." She was very near tears.

Will Stuart clapped his head against his forehead, exasperated with himself. He had been a little uneasy about Billy's disappearance, but Peter Ward had driven it from his mind. Now it was dark, and any search would be difficult. And he was tired.

"I want you to call the police," she said.

"Oh, come on, Beth, that'll not be needed."

"It will," she said firmly, "there's something wrong."

"I'll go out with the van and have a look around. Did you call Joanna Gibbon?"

"Yes, they've not seen him for weeks."

"Of course, he fell out with Geordie, over the dog."

"It's that dog," Beth Stuart said. "He got – he got awful tied up with it." She bit her lip. "He got that strange. He's not been right since he lost it. He was – kind of obsessed."

"I know." Will Stuart looked thoughtful. "He's nearly fifteen. He can look after himself. When I was that age—"

"That's nonsense. There's something *wrong*." She was quite adamant. "I nursed him through that fever, that night when he went out – to look. You've no notion what it was like. I thought he was going to go out of his head altogether."

"You never called the doctor."

"Ach, doctors." She turned away impatiently. After a pause, she said, "Well, are you going then?"

"Yes, I'll go. I'll go along Pitmullen way."

"Do that. Call Rob. He wants to go with you."

Will Stuart knew it was going to be impossible. They scoured every road, turned the van into every gate to shine the headlamps over the fields. They called out till they were hoarse. They searched round the Bing. There was nothing. It brought home to them how little they knew of the places Billy went.

Next morning Will Stuart consented to call the police. The news chased round the neighbourhood hard on the heels of the news about the Yard and Peter Ward's death. Some tried to make connections, but their imaginations were stretched.

The police asked questions, questions. Beth thought they seemed to have much more energy for searching their minds than the fields and woods all around. Had Billy ever run away before? Had he ever talked about it? Did he have any favourite relatives who lived out of the area? Did he want to go to London? Had he been alone? Did he have any special friends? Who had seen him last?

Billy's only special friend had been Geordie

Gibbon; and Geordie no longer knew anything about Billy. His only other special friend had been a dog, and it was dead. The person who had seen him last was also dead.

They tried to track Billy's movements from Peter Ward's hut, but he had left no trail that man or dog could pick up. If he had let go of Peter Ward's wheelbarrow and flown up into the trees he could not have left less trace of himself.

Tuesday passed, and Wednesday. Everywhere the searchers drew a blank. Groups of neighbours got themselves together to search. Even Dave Simmers joined in.

Thursday passed slowly. Peter Ward's funeral was one of the biggest anyone in the neighbourhood remembered. The warm spell broke. A biting dry wind and overcast sky came in from the north-west.

Package 10

Hobart
August 12, 1984

Dear Roger,

There's another bit omitted from the
diary this time - you'll see where it
is. The only reason I've left it out is
that it covers the same ground as the
story - the chapter enclosed and the
next chapter (to follow soon). The
diary account was a bit scrappy, and
confusing, and I actually still remember a lot more about the whole business
than I wrote down at the time.

    The bit of the diary that *is* enclosed
should give you a bit of a laugh. A
memorable night in the history of a
Certain Young Man, I should say!

A.E.

T.T.

DIARY

June 29th, 1974

Everything's changed. I mean, really drastically changed. I don't know if I'll see Billy again, I don't know if I could. Properly, I mean. I saw him on Monday. That was three days after it happened. It was on the school bus, when I couldn't really avoid him. I was determined to stay really cool, but friendly too. But he hardly even looked at me. He told me what had happened after we split up, but there was no real communication: neither of us could talk about the thing we really wanted to talk about.

I still don't really understand what happened, or what I feel for him, or anything.

No, I don't want to write about that just now.

Everything's changed with Mum and Dad of course, that's partly what's confusing me about Billy. Before, when I felt that Mum didn't want me to have anything to do with him, and I wasn't allowed to do what I wanted at weekends and that – I was desperate to be with him. But now that I've talked about him so much with Mum, I feel different. I still like him, but...

If I'd tried to make Mum see my point of

view, I'd have made a total mess of it, I'd never have managed. I'd have got all tied up about starting the conversation in the first place, and then the first thing she said against me, I'd have gone to pieces and started screaming at her or something. It worked because complete strangers were on my side – well, not exactly on my *side*. But I realize it was because of those policemen that Mum got a sense of perspective which she didn't have before. Living here on the farm – not seeing that many people – I know she goes into Blackhall for messages, and to the church – I think she's become sort of isolated from real life. And probably she's like Dad and doesn't notice the years passing either. She was probably still living in the time when I was just four or five and crawling around under her feet.

Billy had set off towards the house, of course, so I made a dash for it in the opposite direction, that's how I ended up on the road. Of course I knew it was late, I knew I was going to be really late back to Jemma's, but it never crossed my mind that she'd let the cat out of the bag. I didn't think the police would be involved. Oh well, I suppose I couldn't really have expected her to tell Mum a pack of lies. Anyway, it all turned out for the best.

This isn't very clear. I'll start at the beginning. Jemma's mum and dad were going away for a long weekend – that was last weekend. So, her mum said they knew they could trust us: we could have friends in, but there wasn't to be any wild parties. It shows how much she did trust us that she didn't even ring Mum up to tell her they weren't going to be there. And I didn't tell Mum of course. I suppose if I hadn't been doing things behind her back anyway I would have told her, but I'd got so into the way of deceiving her, I never even thought about it. I'm sorry about that now – I think it really hurt her – and I don't feel the way I used to, that it was her own fault for not letting me have my freedom. I'm sure I could have handled things better, *somehow*.

Anyway, Jemma was going to have Angela and Jake over, and Roger for herself, and Billy and me. Billy had his house key, so it didn't matter when he got back, and Roger was all right too. Angela and Jake had to be home by one o'clock, but the rest of us could have as much time as we wanted. I was really looking forward to it, but I felt a bit scared as well. Just a bit. It was just – well, I didn't know exactly how far I wanted to *go* with Billy, and I was sort of scared we might get carried away, and – I mean, up to then, it was probably more that we'd never had a proper opportunity. Not like Jemma and Roger.

So we all met up at Jemma's. Roger and
Jake had brought some beer. Thank God I
didn't have any of that. Billy won't touch the
stuff. It's funny that, considering he's been
going into pubs since he was twelve, but he
says he's not interested. Maybe he's seen too
much of the results of it. Jemma told me
Angela was sick, and Jake was lucky he
wasn't. So Billy said let's go out for a walk,
and I wanted to go anyway because it was
such a lovely night, with a really bright
moon. I'd had a cigarette, and I felt a bit
dizzy.

We went to the end of Jemma's road, out
to the fields. Billy suddenly said, Let's walk
over to the wood. Which wood? I said.
Drift's wood, he said, as if I should have
known all the time. I said, It's three miles
from Couston to Pitmullen – that's a six-mile
walk. (It doesn't sound all that far, I suppose,
but I had my tight shoes on.) But he said,
There's plenty of time, we can rest there. I
looked up at the moon – at the moonlight
covering everything with its soft, secret light:
it was a warm night and there was some kind
of scent in the air – I suppose out of the gardens. I thought how lovely it would be to go
to that secret place – I could see it in my
mind, like a bowl full of moonlight. So I said
OK, and we stepped out.

It felt like hours before we got there.

Of course, we hadn't told Jemma where
we were going or how long we'd be. So she'd
already been wondering what had happened
to us when Mum rang her up. God knows
why she did – mother's instinct or something.
She'd never *normally* have rung up to say I'd
left my toothbrush behind, even though I
don't think I ever actually have, before. And
then the way she went on at Jemma, trying to
get out of her why I'd gone out of the house
and Jemma was left in it. Then she asked to
speak to her mother, and Jemma had to say
she'd gone away: and her dad too. I can just
imagine the reactions! Jemma said she went
spare.

Funny to think I was just down at the
other end of the track the whole time – Mum
could just about have seen me if she'd looked
out of my bedroom window. But of course
she didn't, and when she got hold of the
police they began by searching all round
Couston (Jemma was *really* sour about that –
she said that if Jake and Angela and Roger
hadn't happened to be out of the way up in
the bedrooms, the police could have got
really awkward when they called. Talk about
being caught with your pants down!)

The police were actually just on their way
to check up with Mum if there was anything
else she could tell them (Dad had been sent
out in the car by this time to look for me

too), when they found me wandering down the road all by myself. At first they thought I was in a state of shock – I suppose I was, in a way. They asked me all kinds of questions – I can't remember exactly what, but I remember thinking that none of their questions seemed to connect up to where I'd been or what I'd been doing.

I realized a bit further on that they thought I'd been raped. I'm glad I didn't give them Billy's name till after I'd realized this and assured them that I hadn't been, or else they'd probably have shot off in a puff of blue smoke to nab him. I told them his name just as we were driving up to the house. When I said "Billy Stuart" the policeman in the passenger seat turned round and gave me a really queer look. I suppose he recognized the name from a year ago – the Disappearance, and the accident. He said, It's a queer kind of place to go courting, isn't it, where someone got killed? I'd never thought of that, and then it suddenly hit me and I saw Billy again the way I'd last seen him, and I felt – I don't know: like someone had thrown a burning cloth over my head or something – enveloped in heat; and then I just burst into tears. So then they let me out of the car and took me inside.

They must have been satisfied with what I'd said, because when we got inside they turned really nice. They said they'd have to see Billy just to hear his story, but what they told Mum was that I'd been for a walk with my boyfriend and that we'd quarrelled and that I was just walking home. I heard all that in a kind of dream, because when I got into the house and saw everything looking so familiar and safe I burst into tears again and just clung onto Mum. She hardly said anything to me while they were there. She was too flabbergasted, I think.

I don't think I'll ever think badly about a policeman. Those two policemen did in about ten minutes what I don't think I could have done in ten years: convinced her that it was perfectly normal, and natural, and – well, respectable, I suppose – that a fifteen-year-old girl should have a boyfriend, should *want* to have a boyfriend of her *own* choice, want to be with him, go out with him, go to discos, stay up late. They said they were always running into courting couples in queer places. It was that phrase "courting couples" – it was amazing what a relief it was to hear them using that phrase, though really I still don't feel it applies to Billy and me. But that's all we were to them, a "courting couple". A well-known category. That's all they needed to know.

In a way, it's because it's a *category* that Mum can understand it too – though there were some things I didn't, and wouldn't, mention to her. She got a bit upset after the policemen left, and I got a bit hysterical. I screamed at her that I was still a virgin and that if she didn't believe me she could get a doctor to come and examine me, and Billy would never have forced himself on me. She said there was no need to talk like that, but it calmed her down a good bit anyway. I suppose she thinks the Working Classes are all animals and are capable of anything.

The police gave Billy a harder time than me, I think, from what I could get out of him. They got him just as he was getting back to his house. They asked him a lot of questions, but they didn't bother his parents when they saw all the lights in the house were off and Billy had a key. I suppose they must think he's a bit of a queer fish anyway. I wonder if his mum lies awake waiting for him. She'd never say if she did.

Dad came in after Mum and I had calmed down a bit. She kept going on about "your poor father, he's worried sick", but as soon as he came in I could see he wasn't worried sick at all. He didn't say anything, he just gave me a long, sad sort of look. I knew what it meant: I gave you the chance to speak, and you didn't, you went behind our backs instead. I just blurted out, I'm sorry, Dad. It was such a relief. He came and stood beside me and stroked my hair. Mum was just starting off again. "Do you know where she was? She was—" but he interrupted her, he said, Aye, aye: where the dog's buried and where the accident was. I realized he'd thought a lot about everything.

Mum calmed down completely after that, and sent me off to bed. I don't know: home seems so safe and – *right.*

Next day we had a long talk, about Billy, and things. I managed to blank off everything that had happened the night before, just as though it didn't exist, and I told her a bit about what I'd felt for him otherwise. I could see she didn't really approve, but she had to accept it, had to accept that I was serious about him. She was very hurt about me and Jemma going out at the weekends without telling her, and I think she was really angry at Jemma's mum too. But she rang her on Monday, and I think they got things straightened out a bit. I wish I could have heard the conversation! Jemma's mum was OK with Jemma too – after all, there hadn't been any wild party! Jemma had got all the beds and everything sorted before her mum and dad came back.

Mum said she was sorry I'd felt I couldn't speak to her freely, and that's a lot for her to admit. She said it was because I was her only daughter and she'd felt really protective. She said both Sam and Ronnie had been really quiet that way – about girls, and going out, and that – when they were still at home, and she'd thought I'd be the same. Of course you're a girl, she said, and you're very pretty, so I suppose it's different with you. I never knew Mum thought I was pretty!

She also said some stuff about Grandad. Not exactly about missing him – I think part of her trouble was that she felt she didn't miss him, and she was bothered because they'd never been close and now there wouldn't be any chance of it any more, and it was all connected up with her and me not getting on because I was growing up and not needing her any more.

So anyway, *that's* all right. It's just: there's a huge part of me... It's like a big black wall. When I come too near it – oh God, my heart-beat goes up to twice its normal and my armpits get all prickly, it's horrible. I can write about anything: except that hour in – You-Know-Where. It's like, whenever I come near the Wood in my mind, something in me screams out: Go away! Keep away from here! Needless to say, I've got off at the proper road-end all week.

Tuesday's the last day of school. I've got to speak to Billy properly. Oh God, and I was *so* looking forward to the holidays with him.

July 5th, 1974

I'm going to have to write about it. I know I have to, but I keep putting it off.

(Two hours later) It all came out. Everything, when we were in the Wood. Billy remembered everything. That's not really the problem – it's what happened afterwards that's the problem. So, I should try and write about the bit that's not the problem. I've been writing everything else down – it's what everything has been leading up to, isn't it – so it would be really odd if I made an exception of the climax. It might even get like I'll make myself forget about it, and then it'll be the story of Billy Stuart all over again, only it'll be Treeza Thain. God knows what'll happen when it finally comes bursting out of *me*. So, I'm going to start now. Just the things Billy remembered, not how he remembered. It wasn't all that easy to make it all out. It came out in little bursts and gasps – almost like he was being sick. And almost as though he was living through it all again.

It doesn't explain anything. There was nothing I could have told the police about it, even if they'd wanted to know – which they don't because that case is closed. It's weird. Last year they thought Billy had been abducted, this year they think I was raped – they're always thinking the worst: but the worst isn't necessarily the most terrible.

After Billy had been up to Grandad's hut – of course, he didn't know he was dead. That was weird too, how that happened, just at the same time. Billy kept saying, The air's all dark. He said: It's because Peter Ward's dying, that's why the air's so dark. It's as if he understood everything. He said: Peter Ward's dying, that's how I could get through...

CHAPTER
9

SHADOWS

Billy knew that the land began to slope down-hill again beyond Peter Ward's hut. But not like this. You would never have said that Peter Ward's hut stood at the top of a hill. It was a land of dips and folds and hollows, where cattle and sheep rambled and hill-birds wheeled, and the stony track meandered up and down and in and out, on its way towards the road.

All that was different now. A hill slanted down in front of him, a straight, smooth, determined slope with a slight convex curve, dwindling down to a dark, narrow slot at least a thousand feet below and possibly two or three miles distant. On the far side of the dark, winding floor of that valley, which might have been a river or might have been a road, a similar hillside rose, smooth and steady.

But it was the colours which first arrested

Billy. To begin with, all had looked merely sombre and colourless after the bright day he had stepped out of. Now he saw that, although muted, the colours of this new landscape were powerful and luminous. The sky dominated all the other colours. It was not grey, as it had looked at first, but a luminous slate-blue that was almost an opal blue. It was like the approach of massive storm clouds on a day when the sun was still shining brightly on the opposite side of the sky. At first Billy thought that was what it was.

He glanced behind him. Behind him there certainly was the day – or the world – he had just left, but now that his eyes were used to that dimmer light ahead of him, the brightness behind him looked merely white, drained of colour. The two did not match up: it was not clouds moving up on a bright sky, it was two different skies, two different worlds. There was a gulf between them almost as if it had been cut across the sky with a knife. Yet he could not see where the two met. One simply receded behind him, the other stretched before him. There was no going back.

Nor did he want to. The colours here were so much richer, dimmer, subtler, more mysterious. The hillside he stood on had a purplish tone to it. It seemed to be covered with a feathery, downy sort of heather, but Billy couldn't make out if the colour were from flowers on it or from the leaves. If it was early July, it couldn't be heather in bloom. But was it still July? It did not occur to him to stoop and examine the heather: he seemed to have come into a world where you could only view things at a distance. Perhaps the colour came from the ground itself and was just shining through the heather.

The far hillside was bluish in colour, though a pinker blue than the sky, and there seemed to be something like cliffs farther down the valley, a deep reddish colour that tricked the eyes.

Billy glanced behind him. He was surprised to see Peter Ward's hut as far away as it was: he did not remember moving down the hill from the corner where he had put down the wheelbarrow. He was surprised, but not alarmed. This new world seemed so much more solid and real than the one he had just left: it seemed logical that Peter Ward's hut should be so far away. The trees around it were hardly visible as trees: they were misty, spiralling shapes with no colour or substance.

Billy seemed to stand on that strange hillside for hours, but he never felt impatient, or had any desire to move. He might almost have been a tree himself. It never occurred to him to move.

But a change came in the air. It was almost, for a moment, as if the sky had frowned. The air darkened, as it had done before that day, back in the old, bright world. For a moment the atmosphere became uncanny, and a dry breeze stirred up out of nowhere and came swishing up the valley through the heather, ruffled Billy's hair, and died away. And down in the valley something was moving.

It was impossible at first to see what it was. It was white, bluish white, like a star that glided over the ground. But it cast no light. Then gradually Billy could see that it must be an animal of some kind: it still glided, but there was a jerk of animal movement about it. It drew nearer.

It was an animal, an animal running. It was not all white: it was an animal composed of light and shadow. The shadow looked merely black at first, but little by little it began to show up a ruddy colour on the purple hillside in the bluish air. It was a dog running, half towards Billy, in a wide circle, low to the ground.

Billy stood rooted. Drift came nearer and nearer, but not straight towards him. It was more as if Billy were a quarry the dog was seeking out – a rabbit, or an errant lamb. Billy could see his eyes glinting. He circled round behind Billy. Billy could not move. He appeared on the other side of him, closed the circle up. Billy found his voice.

"Drift." The name came out hoarsely. Drift

dropped to the ground, flat down, his nose pointing towards Billy, chin flat to the ground.

"Drift," Billy called again. "Here, Drift."

Drift raised his head and panted. But he did not move. He was different.

It was the strangest moment of all. On the one hand, the face was so familiar to Billy that in comparison every other face he knew seemed like the face of a stranger. It was nearer and more familiar than Drift's face had ever been in his life – more familiar than his mother's or his father's, or Geordie's or Rob's or Liz's. On the other hand it was wholly alien: it could not have been more alien if he had been a creature dropped from another star.

"Drift?" Billy said again, uncertainly.

Drift rose. Billy held out his hand. But then Drift turned, and began to trot back the way he had come. Still it did not occur to Billy to move from the spot he was on. But at about fifty yards' distance, Drift paused and looked back at him, his tongue lolling. The bluish light seemed all around him. And suddenly, after hours of standing, Billy's body seemed to come to life for him again. He walked. He began to jog along the hillside, following Drift. The dog did not turn down the hill; he ran along it, parallel to the valley down on their left. But it was so easy to jog along, the land must have been falling gently all the time. It was in fact some while before Billy realized that they were on a path of dry earth, hard-packed. It was a rich reddish brown that seemed to catch the light and glow faintly with it.

The track became wider, well trodden. Suddenly Drift turned round and lay facing Billy. He felt the urgent command to stand still, and stood. Just ahead of him, another track crossed the track they were on: a wider, double track. Drift lay on the far side of it.

For a long time nothing happened. The dusk seemed to be deepening. Billy and Drift remained motionless, each gazing at the other. Then at last there came a sound from the hillside above them, to Billy's right – a slow, heavy thud-thud, a creaking and squeaking, a regular, swishing sound. Billy's heart began to beat fast.

Two huge shapes loomed out of the other track above them. At first, in the gloom, it looked like two misshapen moons rising side by side. As they became clearer, Billy saw that it was two white oxen, vast brutes with yard-long horns pointing forwards like bicycle handlebars turned around. Something was dragging behind them. Their heavy footsteps seemed quieter now that they were nearer. What you heard was the rustle and jog of their heavy bodies, and the breath blowing from their nostrils.

They came alongside. They were not sleek,

they had curly hair between their horns and along their sides down to the edge of their bellies. Their necks were thicker than tree trunks, the great pouch of fat swaying under them down to between their forelegs. Each wore a harness of twisted yellowish rope, and they were dragging behind them a kind of wicker sledge drawn on brushwood runners. These were making the regular, swishing sound Billy had first heard. There was a shape on the sledge: though Billy was not able to make it out over the basketlike edges, he thought it seemed like the shape of someone stretched out on his back.

The oxen and sledge passed slowly, creaking and dwindling downhill. Not until they had vanished into the dusk would Drift rise and turn and let Billy follow.

So they continued, and now the downhill slope began to be more pronounced. After a long while they had to stop again and wait while two oxen and a sledge – possibly the same one, possibly another – came at the same stately pace uphill out of the valley.

Now Billy saw that the opposite hillside, as he had thought, fell away here and there into steep cliffs. They were now much nearer the deep slot in the floor of the valley. It was not like going down into an ordinary valley, where the silence of the hills gradually becomes crowded out by the multitude of small low-

241

land sounds. Here, the silence continued unabated.

The darkness grew, but there was still a quality of distinctness about the light, and Billy could make out details. They came to the floor of the valley, a broad, stone-strewn road. From where they stood it dipped swiftly down between cliffs. Drift led Billy down it.

It was hard going. Billy kept tripping on stones, or stepping on them and turning his ankle. Drift drew further away from him.

They came out of the steep space between cliffs to a part where the hillsides on either hand fell more gently and the valley bed broadened out. In that wide space a crowd of people was gathered.

By a trick of the dim, distinct light, Billy for a moment actually thought that they were sheep. There was something sheeplike in the way the majority of them were huddled in a bunch, while at the fringes they were more scattered about and might almost have been grazing. Drift stopped when he saw them, and Billy had to stop too. He could not see them clearly. They all looked very pale. Some seemed to be wearing tunics or dresses, some shirts and trousers, but they were all in the same beige-yellow cloth, similar to the colour of the oxen's harness ropes.

Drift stood and surveyed them. Those at the centre huddled closer, while those at the fringes drifted a little towards the main crowd.

Suddenly Drift darted out to the right, semi-circling round the outriders there. Without a sound they ran in to huddle at the centre. Drift looped back and sprinted round those still scattered on the left side. They, too, crowded in to the main body. His intention was plain, as he darted back and forth. The crowd of people turned and started to move slowly down the valley, stumbling on the stones just as Billy had done.

Now and then the silence broke a little with a soft murmuring from the crowd of people. But they would soon fall silent again. It was a strange procession, Drift running to and fro behind them, as if putting on his very best per-formance for some important shepherd. Yet Billy was not the shepherd: in his own way he was as much under Drift's power as the people the dog was herding.

The darkness did not seem to be growing any more. It had settled in a constant dusk. But Billy saw that ahead the sky was utterly black. They were moving down from a land of per-petual dusk to a land of perpetual night. Soon they would come to a boundary between the two.

And so they did.

On either side of the road, set well back from it on the first slopes of the hillsides, Billy saw two rough stone pillars. They were about man-height, upright, silver-grey. Beyond them there was pitch-black night.

Between those gateposts the crowd halted, and a murmuring began.

On impulse, Billy looked behind. High in the air over the road he saw a small white cross. It grew. It was a bird, shining so whitely it looked as though the daylight sun must be catching it from another world. The bird glided down, and for a moment alighted on the right-hand stone. It was a curlew, but white to the very tip of its long curved beak. Against the night ahead it shone like a piece of the moon. It called out once: not a curlew's yodelling cry but a sharp, clean call. And then it flew up, spanning the air over the left-hand pillar and then on, vanishing up over the steep hillside on the left.

Still the people murmured, and heads were being turned, following the path the white bird had taken. Billy looked up, too, but could see nothing. He noticed that Drift was lying now, pointed in the same direction, in his attitude of silent command.

At last Billy saw. There was a figure up on the hillside, a figure so dim it was hard to make out against the rocks that were littered about at that point. It had apparently been quite still, but now that everyone was watching it started moving. A little aimlessly: back, away from the darkness, up a little, as if wanting to climb

244

out of the valley. At once Drift hurtled forwards. He covered that five minutes' climb in about thirty seconds, his bounding shape soon disappearing from sight and becoming, again, a white spot that glided irregularly over the ground. Billy was struck by how clearly defined the figure on the hillside was by comparison. Drift encircled it, and began to drive it down, unwillingly as it seemed, towards the others.

It seemed to be the figure of a young man, who tripped and fell awkwardly several times as he clambered down the hillside. He came to a stop a little way from the crowd of people. Drift rushed in, snapping at his heels, but the young man did not move. Again he rushed in, but again the stranger stood his ground. He would go so close to the others, but no closer. Drift let him be.

All the others had turned back to the road now, and seemed ready to move on again. Drift again began his quick semicircular trot behind them, and they began to move between the wide gateposts down into the darkness. For a moment the young man hesitated, then he, too, followed, still keeping his distance. Drift let him be. Half the company had passed through. Now only twenty were left. Now only five. The young man came to the edge of the darkness. There he paused and looked back, and for the first time Billy saw his face.

He knew the face was familiar, but it was so sad and pale, glanced at him so woefully, that for a moment he couldn't think who it was. Suddenly he realized, and gave a start, and all the hair prickled up the back of his neck. It was Dave Simmers.

It was almost as if that recognition was what the young man had been waiting for. Dave Simmers turned, and followed the crowd into the night. Drift came on behind, and Billy followed Drift.

It was as he had expected. As soon as he had passed the gate, deep dusk suddenly became unlimited night. However, he could still make out the others, although only dimly. The pale heads of the people showed up, not as individual heads but like ripples of water. He could still make out Dave Simmers, just, at the rear and to the left. Drift was more distinct, two bobbing patches of white, one for his white ruff one for the tip of his tail. Billy kept his eyes on that: it made it easier as he fumbled his way forward in the solid blackness.

But it was slow, and he kept knocking his feet painfully against the stones he couldn't see. And he seemed to be getting slower: or else Drift and his quiet flock were getting quicker. At any rate they were drawing away from him. Drift's two patches merged into a single patch. He could see no sign of Dave Simmers.

He tried to hurry, but no effort seemed to

bring them any closer. He could hardly see the one patch of white any more.

He fell. He must have tripped over a stone, though he hadn't felt it. He fell forward onto his hands and knees, grazing them painfully. He struggled to his feet as fast as he could, but his body felt like lead. "Drift," he whispered. "Drift. Drift." But there was nothing.

Still the darkness was not total. He could see his hand, or almost see it. There was the faintest of faint light coming from the hills. Not near to, but further up, receded in the high darkness on either side. A whiteness on the hills, a tricking gleam that might almost have been his imagination. For the first time, Billy felt cold. Could it be snow, up there on the higher part of the hills?

No, not snow, he thought to himself as the faint whiteness tricked and glimmered there. Not snow: the hills are made of bone. "The hills are made of bone," he whispered aloud, as if to comfort himself. He tripped again, not over a stone this time but over his own leaden feet. He fell full-length and lay with his cheek against the rough stones. The blackness entered him.

Package 11

Hobart

Dear Roger,

This is the other bit of the story that
covers the same ground as the diary.
And then, the very last bit of my poor
dismembered diary itself…

T.T.

CHAPTER
10

THE HUNT

It was slightly less dark when Billy awoke, but the cold was worse than ever. He felt the road hard under him. It looked paler: perhaps his eyes were more used to it. He looked up to see if the hills of bone were any clearer. There was no sign of them. Something reared over him still, but it didn't seem like rock-wall: it was like clouds of black against something paler, with bold black lines and sharp angles here and there. It took him some time to realize he was looking at the night sky through a screen of trees.

He struggled to his feet. He was both stiff and trembling with the cold, and his legs still seemed unwilling to carry him. Yet there was also a strange burning feeling at the root of his spine, and occasionally stabs of pain flared up his back. He took steps forward, slowly, stiffly. Six steps. An upright thing glimmered, a T-shaped thing, beside the road. He stared at it blankly for some minutes, shivering, before he realized it was a signpost. One arm read: BUCKSBURN 7 MILES. The other: DAVIEBURN 7 MILES.

The shivering turned to sobbing. He had felt no fear while in the strange dim landscape where Drift still ran; but to see that name: DAVIEBURN – home – overwhelmed him with relief and pity for himself. He could not think of walking that distance on his stiff and unresponsive legs. Almost he could have clutched and hugged the signpost, almost as if it had been the thing itself and not just a reminder of how far home was.

A low, familiar-sounding hum made him start and listen. At the same time the flares of pain shot up his back and into his neck, making him tilt his head back sharply so that sparks of light stabbed at his eyes. The pain died back into that knot of heat in the base of his spine, but the lights in his eyes steadied, and grew broader, like a swift dawn. The humming grew louder. The light separated into two pale fans that flicked with shadow, and it was only then that he understood that it was a car approaching.

It was still some way off when the fan of light swept him. He saw then that the signpost stood at the junction of three roads, and there was a third arm pointing up the road he had, apparently, come from: BLACKHALL 7 MILES. He took this information in slowly, and tried for the first time to think how he had got here. And where he was. The main road to Edinburgh was the road which took you from Blackhall to Bucksburn: but he was on a small country road. And what was this thing about seven miles? It was almost like a joke.

He only gradually became aware that he was standing in the full glare of the light and the car had come to a stop near him. He saw the outline of a door opening, and then heard a dim voice: "Billy? Billy Stuart?" Then a shadow came between him and the light, a tall, broad shape. Another flare of pain shot up his back, died away again into that burning knot. "Where have you been, for Christ's sake?" the voice said. "They've been looking for you for days – the fuzz and all."

Billy didn't answer. A more urgent question had shaped itself in his mind: where had he heard that voice before? Who did it belong to? There was something in that voice that made his mind buzz with danger.

He hit it a split second before the head turned side-on to the light and he saw the silhouette. And having seen it, he had reached the ditch in a single bound and was diving for the fence and the shadow of the trees before he had even shaped the name of the danger – pure instinct, like a hare in flight. He felt a sudden sharp delight in being able to stretch his muscles again, to run freely. He was through the fence, weaving between beech trunks silver in the car lights. There were heavy footfalls behind him. Another fence appeared: he took it in a single vault, with all the dark space of fields before him...

"Got you!" Billy felt his armpits wrenched back, a fist gripping fast onto the back of his shirt. He was on one side of the fence, his pursuer on the other. He struggled, but another hand twined itself in his hair, dragging him backwards against the fence. The pursuit had been more desperate than the flight. His head was pulled backwards over the fence wire.

Dave Simmers' face, upside down, in the sharp light and shadow of the car headlights, was nothing short of demonic. Billy winced with the pain in his neck. "I'm just trying to get you home." Dave Simmers ground out the words between gritted teeth.

"Let go of me," Billy muttered. Somehow, he wasn't speaking to Dave Simmers: he was speaking to two hands which were holding him by the shirt and the hair, and to a barbed-wire fence which was digging into his back. The hand in his hair was making his eyes run.

Then his shirt was released, one leg was grabbed, and he was swung backwards over the fence, pivoting on a knee like a hay bale, and landed onto the ground. And now he fought. He lashed out wildly, impersonally. The arm, the leg, the stomach, whatever seemed to be in reach. The hand pressed down on his head, and his knees buckled. As he slipped down, Dave Simmers' knees came down onto his chest, subsided onto him, crushing him into the grass.

Still Billy fought, but still the hand held tight to his hair. He still struggled on when the fist appeared in front of his face, but when it came smashing down onto his cheekbone and the side of his nose, he let himself go limp. He was rolled over, picked up by his hair and the belt of his jeans, and carried through the trees, over the other fence, and to the car. He was sobbing with the pain in his head, but he would not let himself cry out.

Dave Simmers let go of Billy's belt, letting him fall but still holding onto his hair, and opened the back door of the car with his free hand. Then he picked Billy up again and flung him face down across the back seat. His hair was freed, and he sobbed with relief.

Dave Simmers knelt on Billy's back, twisted his arms up behind him, and began to lash them together at the wrists. It was plastic baler-twine by the feel, sharp, cutting into his skin. After the wrists, his ankles were secured. The back door shut, the car rocked as Dave Simmers let himself into the driver's seat. The car was jolted into gear. They gathered speed.

253

Immobilized in the back of the car, Billy sobbed, then panted, then quietened. At last he began to feel, to think, to be awake. Where had he been? What had been happening? Who was this Dave Simmers and what was happening now? For now the strangeness of everything poured in on him. There were two Dave Simmers: one the bully, the manipulator, the ugly thing he had always known and feared; the other, the strange, sad creature whom Drift had herded, faltering and unwilling, into the blackness of that other place. The two were here, together, in this one car – one just across the barrier of the seats, crunching gears, squealing brakes, driving like a mad thing, muttering and cursing, one within him, in a dim, silent, utterly peaceful place. Now Dave Simmers was the hare; Billy had come to rest. And the knot in the base of his spine was released. Heat was pouring upwards, slowly, irresistibly, towards his head.

They hurtled round a corner, and Billy was half-thrown from his seat. He sat up, bent forwards to accommodate his tied hands. Giant beech trees loomed in the headlights, loomed and flicked past, loomed and flicked past. He was thrown from side to side, unable to steady himself.

"What are you doing, Davie?" he asked at last, quietly and steadily. "Why have you tied me up? Where are you taking me?"

"Hold your tongue! Shut up! Lie down!" Dave Simmers screamed, lashing backwards at him with his arm but only hitting the seat. The car swerved and their wild career continued, and so did Simmers' screaming. "See you, you little bastard? I could kill you. You'd bloody deserve it. Your dad too. I'll bloody kill him. He's got everything that's coming to him. Everything! Do you hear me?"

The heat was concentrated in the middle of Billy's back, but from the waist down he felt cold, stone-cold. Suddenly he felt incomprehensible, overwhelming pity for his captor. He had never felt anything like it in his life, not even when he had come upon the dog dead in the ground and realized it was Drift. He seemed to be looking down at Dave Simmers from a great height as he clutched desperately at the wheel of an uncontrolled car, looking down as if at an insect drowning in a puddle. "Oh, Davie," he groaned, not knowing what he was saying, "let go, man, it'll be all right – you'll be quite safe."

Dave Simmers let go the wheel with one hand, turned to Billy, seized his whole face in the free hand and flung him over onto his side again. He braked hard and the car swerved viciously again. The headlights of an oncoming car had thrown him off his bearings. "One more word," he screamed, "just – just one more word!"

The moment was past. Pushing himself up again with his elbows, Billy felt the heat reach between his shoulder blades. Dave Simmers would have to take whatever was coming to him. "Not me, and not my dad," Billy whispered. "It's you, Davie, you."

Dave Simmers did not answer. Open farmland went past, a blur of hawthorn hedges. A darker patch loomed ahead – woods again, on either side of the road. The heat surged into the back of Billy's head. Himself was forgotten. His own fate was unimportant. The insect was drowning. The heat burst against the roof of his head.

Billy forced himself upright, standing, his head pressed against the roof of the car, holding himself rigid. The power was tremendous. He was rigid with it, like a bolt of icy steel. He felt his plastic bonds melting away, but made no attempt to move arms or legs from their locked position. "Now, Dave Simmers! Now, boy!"

Dave Simmers' hands flew from the steering wheel. For a moment he seemed to be trying to turn to Billy. Then he seemed to catch sight of something on the road ahead. It all happened in split seconds. He was slamming on the brakes, screaming and cursing as the tyres screamed on the road, but his hands were off the wheel, covering his head, covering his eyes. Billy had a brief image of trees waving madly

256

in a gale. Then the impact, the rending and splintering. Great hands seemed to lay hold of him, ejecting him through the open back door, rolling him over and over on the verge. His last image, before darkness fell, was of the back of the car bursting open, and white birds flying up from it, up into the branches of the trees.

Then there was silence, darkness and silence, for what seemed a long time but must have been only seconds. Billy became aware of himself again, lying half on his front, half on his side, in the grass. He was emptied. He knew the warm stuff pouring over his left eye, dimming his sight, was blood. It didn't worry him. There had been elation, now there was exhaustion. Nothing matters, he thought, breathing the free air; nothing matters now.

Through the grass-blades he caught a glimpse of the Dog slinking back in between the trees,white patches, dark patches, merging into the tree-shadow. Wolflike, head hanging, tongue hanging out over the lower teeth, casting over his shoulder that shifty, half-complacent glance... Eternally seeking praise, eternally expecting a blow, man's shadow, Dog as he had been for hundreds and thousands of years: the quarry hunted and brought to the ground, the stray sheep encircled and brought back to the flock.

Billy rose to his feet, and followed.

DIARY

...He was walking up and down and sort of running his fingers through his hair and shaking his head in this really weird way, but when he said how he'd seen Drift there – or not really Drift but a dog anyway that was supposed to be the same as Drift – he suddenly got calmer and came and sat down again and kept taking big, long breaths like really deep sighs. I think I'd realized by this time how the chicken factory place all tied up with it, and how that was the thing that eventually sort of opened the door so he could start remembering. Dave Simmers must have been coming back from the chicken factory with some hens he'd stolen. It was his brother who actually stole the hens from the place where he worked, Dave Simmers just transported them and sold them. And the reason why Billy got such a shock that time outside the factory in Bucksburn when we saw Dave Simmers' brother wasn't because he knew who he was: it was because, seeing someone very like Dave Simmers, but not quite like him – it wasn't so much like a ghost – well, it was, in a way – but it was more because it sort of jolted the memory of what he'd seen back in that Other Place. He'd remembered about the white birds for some reason, and I think he might have remembered about the baler twine, but he couldn't get it all fitted – it wasn't until he realized the white birds were actually the hens escaping and tied that up with the brother and the chicken factory that the whole memory started piecing itself together again. I think it's really amazing.

July 6th, 1974

This isn't actually a new entry. I've been writing all night and it's broad daylight now, though the sun isn't up yet. Actually it's still very early in the morning. But I'm going to go on. If I can't write about it at sunrise in the middle of summer I'll never be able to write about it.

I'd realized by now that he'd got it all out, and after a bit he lay back, quite quietly, and just stared up at the moon. I did the same, for quite a long time. After a bit I went over to him and lay with my arm sort of over him and stroked his face a bit. Then that made me want to start kissing him, so I did, but then he suddenly jumped up again. I got up after him and said sorry – I thought it was my fault – and asked if he was all right. He just shook his head – but it wasn't so much as if he was answering me, it was more as

259

though he was trying to shake something out of it. That started making me feel a bit weird again about the heat thing in his back, and I kept saying, It's all right, it's all right – I think it was more to myself than to him. It was really bright, with the moon and the summer night, everything was almost like daylight, the trees weren't just black like they are at night, you could almost see the red-brown of their trunks and the green of their leaves.

Suddenly I saw a shadow on Billy's forehead. I couldn't understand what it was, I just knew it shouldn't be there. It reminded me of something and I didn't like it. I looked at him closer, went right up to him, and it wasn't there any more. His face looked very pale and his eyes were very dark, but I thought that was just the light. Now he asked me, what's the matter? I said I'd thought there was a mark on his forehead, but there wasn't. So I said I'll kiss it away, but he didn't lower his head for me to reach it. I went up very close to him and put my arms round him, and he put his arms round me, and I was kissing his neck and running my hands up and down his back. Well, I know he likes that – it's not like it was at the very start when I didn't know if he liked the way I feel. I know he likes it, because he gets excited and that and I can *feel* him, and

that's all – all right. Was. Used to be. But
tonight none of this was happening.

And then I put my hands inside his shirt
and – it was horrible, his skin was completely
cold – it was like clay, like something dead. I
said, Billy, what's the matter with you,
you're cold. He said, I'm fine, but there was
something strange about his voice. I took my
hands out of his shirt and stepped back a
little. He looked incredibly pale. Do you not
feel well? I said. He shook his head again:
I'm OK. His hands didn't feel cold, but then
he wasn't actually touching my skin. I put
my hands up to his neck – and it was burning. I went on holding it, because I was sort
of fascinated I suppose – I'd never felt skin
that hot before – and then suddenly it went
completely cold. I mean suddenly, instanta-
neously, as if it had been switched off. I
gripped his neck and stared at him in amazement. Billy! I said. But he was looking
upwards, at the sky.

Then two things happened. The first was,
that dark shadow appeared on his forehead
again – not suddenly, but as if it had spread
or flowed down from his hair. It looked a bit
like a cap. And the other thing was, a wind
got up. That was awful, really awful, I can't
describe it. One moment everything had been
as still as still, not a breath stirring; the next,
the trees were shaking and waving like mad

and there was this roaring wind all around,
things – leaves, I suppose – getting blown
wildly all over the place, the whole wood
shaking and groaning. And of course the first
thing I thought was that it was just like he'd
been telling me about. It's like it had all been
waiting somewhere up the road – at the
seven-mile signpost or somewhere – and as
soon as he started blurting it all out it had all
come alive again and started coming down
the road towards us, as though he'd called it
up. That's what I *actually felt*: I'm not
making it up now. I tried to let go of Billy,
but it seemed ages before I could get my
hands to move, they felt as if they were glued
to his neck, and so heavy. I screamed at him,
Stop it, Billy! – I don't know why but I was
sure it was him. But he said: I can't, it's you,
you're making me. I think I went a bit hysterical then, screaming and stuff, I don't remember much about it.

What happened next was the worst thing. I
still don't know if it was just that I'd sunk
down onto my knees – it could have been. At
any rate, I was looking up at him – I mean,
as though he was a couple of feet above me –
and I was convinced that he was actually
floating above the ground. Then I realized
that the dark cap thing on his forehead was
blood, and his expression was exactly the
same as it had been in those awful night-

mares I used to have about him. And at that moment – it was almost as though he'd *heard* what I'd been remembering, about the nightmares – he started off up the track to the house, and I can't *really* remember, but I'm sure, I'm *sure* he wasn't walking on the ground, in fact I could swear he wasn't walking at all, not moving his legs. And the wind went with him – all round him, as if he were dragging it along behind him. After a bit the wood went quiet, and soon I couldn't see him or even hear him any more. It was eerie. As soon as it was quiet, I made a dash for the road. I don't know where I thought I was going – just the opposite direction from him, that was enough.

There, I've done it. It wasn't so bad after all. I see now that one of the reasons I had to get it written down is I know that, if I don't, I'm simply not going to believe it happened. It sounds so totally weird, like a dream or a horror movie. But it happened. I'm not saying I've described everything accurately – I don't think I was in a fit state to be completely clinical about it: but *something* happened, and I've written it down as I remember it. I can't explain anything about any of it, and I don't think I really want to try to. I suppose there must be books about weird things that happen – well, I don't want to see them. And I'm no nearer knowing

what I feel about him. I don't *want* to see
him again, but I feel I have to. In some way, I
feel it was all my fault. What did he mean, I
was making him? Is that what I've been
doing all along? Whose obsession has it been
– the trips to Bucksburn and everything – his
or mine?

I'm too tired to think now. It's half past
five. I'm going to get a couple of hours' sleep.

July 17th, 1974

Saw him. We were sort of thrown together,
but I'm glad. We got a chance to talk. I think
there's a lot of things clearer in my mind
now. I was in Blackhall with Mum. This was
earlier today. I was to meet up with her in an
hour. I'd just worked out I didn't have
enough money for a Coke *and* the jukebox,
and I wasn't going to have the music without
the Coke or the Coke without the music, so I
was going away from the café over to the
library when I saw Billy coming out of it.
The library, I mean – you could have
knocked me down with a feather.

I do sometimes read, he said. He had a
book in a plastic bag, and I could see he
didn't want to show it to me. It just shows
how much things have changed: before, I'd
have teased him till he did show it to me.

Now, I didn't feel easy enough with him to
tease him. He offered to buy me a Coke, so I
got to the café after all. We sat in the end
corner. The partition cut us off completely
from the rest of the café. We were alone. He
said, Is it still the same with us? I wasn't sure
what he meant – after all, we hadn't spoken
for three weeks. I just said I didn't know.
You think I'm a freak, he said. He wasn't
accusing me, he wasn't bitter, he just said it. I
didn't know what I was wanting to say. I
was just looking over this huge dull yellow
sea (the table) that was stretching and
stretching in front of me, with Billy a thousand miles away on the far horizon; two
black rocks that were our Cokes, mountains
over on the edge where the salt and pepper
and vinegar were. I was just looking at that
as though there was nothing else in the world
for me to look at. I wanted – oh, so badly –
to wrench myself away from it, but I just
didn't seem to know how to.

Suddenly I said – it didn't even seem to be
me that was saying it – I just wanted a
boyfriend, that's all. It seems such an obvious
thing to say, really silly, in fact: but I'd never
quite thought of it like that before. And
saying it, just out of the blue like that – it
was such a relief. I felt something had gone
ping! inside me and suddenly freed me of the
weight that had been lying on my mind. Now

265

that I'm writing this, I'm not sure if that's
really true, somehow. There's still a funny
way I feel guilty – perhaps feel I'm the one
that's the freak. But anyway, that's how I
think I felt then. And he looked at me – he
looked so strange and woeful – and said,
And that's not what I am? And it all suddenly seemed so clear to me, and I said, I'm
sorry but I've got too much competition.
What do you mean? he said. Well, I said – I
hardly even needed to stop and think, it all
seemed so clear – there's two things wrong
with me: one's that I'm not a dog, and the
other's that I'm not dead. I'm trying to think
if I meant this cruelly. It looks like it when
it's written down – not just because of Drift,
because of Dave Simmers as well.

There was a long silence then. I think he
was a bit stunned by what I'd said. At last I
said, I just want to be friends. What do you
mean? he said. God, males! I said, I'd like to
be able to talk to you, to see you now and
again, perhaps we could go for a walk
together sometimes or maybe to a dance or
the café, and all that. But I don't want to *go
out* with you. I like you an awful lot, but I
don't love you. God, I was so definite! What
I didn't say was that I was simply terrified
that every time I put my arms round him,
that same thing *might* just happen like it happened three weeks ago – that cold, dead feel

266

and everything else. Then I said I had to go and meet Mum. I got up, then I thought, why not? and I said, Don't you want to come and see her too? That really caught him on the hop. He blushed, then I blushed too and I got really annoyed. She won't eat you! I almost shouted at him. He grinned, and he came with me. And we met her. Well – there was nothing to say. Billy said hello and was completely tongue-tied. Mum went scarlet and said hello and tried really hard to be natural, but I could see she was rigid with the effort. She said, Well, Billy, you'll have to come round some time and – play records with Theresa. I could have died laughing. I suppose that's what Mum thinks the Younger Generation do. Well, if they aren't running around losing their virginity. I mean, what else *is* there to do?

Package 12

Hobart
August 21, 1984

Dear Roger,

What I sent you in the last package was
actually the last entry in that diary.
It's the end of the story. That's why
I'm not going to start screaming at you
again for commenting between chapters,
although that last chapter wasn't what
I'd planned as the ending. What I'm
sending you now is actually a bit of a
cop-out: I wanted it to be a chapter to
wind everything up, but I didn't really
know how to. What I've enclosed are my
various attempts. I suppose you could
put them all together and call them the
real last chapter – of the Drift-and-
Billy story, that is, but of course
that's just the beginning of the
Treeza-and-Billy story.

Before I go ahead and try and answer
your accusations, I just want to say
how great it's been having had your
attention through all this. Somehow it's
been really necessary for me, I don't
know why. You've been a real friend.

Now, about your criticism. I suppose
I could take them as a compliment
really rather than a criticism - except
that for me, the thing the story's
about, what I've had to say - me, *me* -
is the important thing, not whether I
can write or have written a good story.
Have another think in six months and
see whether you still think it was a
good story, or if it isn't just that
you have a friendly involvement in me.

The thing is, you're quite right: I
did write the story on the scantiest of
information. Billy Stuart never talked
a lot, not even during our best time.
So - how do I have so much detail about
him, his family, etc., etc. Well, the
obvious answer is, I made it up. Cynic
that you are, that's probably the only
explanation that you'd accept.

However, it wouldn't be the truth.
The truth is that I picked up a lot
about Billy's life from hints he gave,
guesses I made - and something extra:
there are things about him that I
simply *know*. I can't tell you how. It's
as though each chance remark, each
grunt of yes or no, each slight inflec-
tion of his voice when he mentioned
something about his family, or Dave
Simmers, or Drift, was like a little

window that he was opening so that I could get a glimpse through it at a whole area of his life – details, far more than he ever said in words.

And I have *total recall*. You've seen for yourself: you've seen my diary (all of it, except that one bit that was irrelevant and that other bit, which just contained a rough description of his account of his "vision" – or whatever it was – and the accident). It was certainly not much to go on. I was piecing Drift's story together in my head all the time I was writing that diary – a year after Drift's story took place – but I didn't bother to write any of it down. And ten years on, I can remember exactly all the little scenes and images just as I could see them then. Do you think it's some special gift I have? If it is, why hasn't it shown itself with anything else in my life?

I say it was something special Billy had. In fact, I'll go further than that: I'll say that *no one* has ever impressed me quite the way Billy Stuart did. There was "something about him" – something you would hardly notice unless you were prepared to look very hard and with a very open mind. It

comes out in the way he was with Drift
- perhaps it was something he got from
Drift. Perhaps it was something he got
from my grandfather too - I don't know
what makes me think that, but I have
this curious sense that Peter Ward
"passed on" something to Billy as he
was dying. I don't know if that's
exactly an explanation for his vision
and his disappearance - five days,
without a single trace - which remain a
total mystery. Of course, it also comes
out in Dave Simmers' death and that
awful experience I had with Billy at
the end. He was bothered that I thought
him a freak; he was also ridden with
guilt about Dave Simmers' death: he
thought he had caused that, and not
just by distracting him from his driving. Dave Simmers *saw* something on the
road ahead. Whatever it was - Drift,
perhaps, or the Dog that was and wasn't
Drift - he felt that *he* had put it
there. Probably he had stopped hating
Dave Simmers right at the end, but he
still felt it was his hatred that had
become like a lethal force.

But whatever happened, anything I
suggest would only reinforce what I'm
saying anyway: Billy Stuart was something very, very special. Not just to

me – OK, he was my first love and all
that, but – not just to me.

The feeling that I have now is: we
did something together. He involved me
in something – perhaps you might call
it a quest, to find out what he'd forgotten – but it was more than that,
too: something that we were working on
side by side, Billy Stuart and I. Looking back, I think I can say it matured
me beyond my years. At the time – you
can see this from my diary – I blew hot
and cold over the whole quest thing.
Yet for all that, I was with him all
the way through. When it came to the
crunch, it wasn't the fact that we'd
got in there – to the bottom of the
secret or the mystery or whatever you'd
call it – it wasn't because of that
that I lost interest in him. It was
what we discovered that I couldn't cope
with. When he said I thought he was a
freak, the honest answer would have
been yes. I couldn't cope. I couldn't
cope with the idea of someone who dis-
appears off the face of the earth and
visits the land of the dead and kills
people with his thoughts. Perhaps I've
spent the last ten years reaching the
stage where I feel I can cope with
that.

And so to the next ten years… You
know, writing about all this – and *to*
someone (ie, you), and reading over my
old diary again and sending it off to
you – oh, I don't know: the whole of
the last four months – it's changed
something in me. Quite radically, I
think. It's really quite strange. I
can't explain *how* it's changed me
exactly, though there's one thing I *can*
put my finger on, and that's that I've
decided not to renew my contract in
Hobart. I'm coming home. Before I
started writing the story, I thought
I'd renew the contract for another two-
year stint, then globe-trot a bit, "do"
the Far East, etc., and perhaps eventually wander home, or somewhere else...

Really, I seriously thought that
writing the story – getting it down on
paper – would be enough; that the whole
exercise would somehow "get it out of
my system", would lay the ghost of
Billy Stuart to rest. Well, it hasn't.
I suppose I suspected it wouldn't.
Anyway, I'm coming straight home. I
must be daft – the contract is to the
end of November, so I'll be back in
time for another blooming winter.

And – yes, I do want to find out
what's happened to him. Mum gives me

the odd bit of local gossip, of course
- like the Bridge Bar closing - but we
never discuss Billy. I don't know what
he's working at, or if he's maybe just
drifting (ha!). I don't know whether
I'll look him up, or just make a few
discreet enquiries. I don't know why I
want to do it, after all these years.
I'd just like to know. No, it goes
deeper than that: I so, so *need* to
know.

Anyway, I should see you before too
long. Keep the manuscript and stuff, if
you don't mind - it cost me a fortune
to send it, and besides, the less I
have to bring back, the better.

Love,

Theresa

CHAPTER
11

BEGINNINGS

"You were no friend of his, Dod, you can't deny it." Hettie put the glass of whisky softly on the bar.

"Nobody's as bad as that," Dod Moffat said.

"He'd tied the laddie up." Hettie was firm, tight-lipped.

"Nobody deserves *that*!" Dod Moffat brought his fist down on the bar, making the glasses jump. "Nobody's that bad. He was bringing young Billy home, that's for certain sure."

"You never know, do you?" Hettie's voice was gentler.

"That's one hundred per cent certain," Dod Moffat said, glowering at Hettie. "They're all the same, women," he muttered. "They can't forgive and forget."

"That's because it's us that has the bairns,"

Hettie retorted. "And that's something men'll never understand."

Dod Moffat sighed. "You never do know, do you." He stared into his whisky. The glass was full of golden light, like an autumn day. "You never know who's pushing someone to do something they don't want to. It's like these terrorists. Most folk are decent, I reckon – ach, you get the odd one that's downright evil – but most folk are decent."

"There's no discipline nowadays, that's what's wrong," Hettie said.

Dod Moffat sighed again. "You're right enough, Henrietta," he said. "I dare say you're right enough."

Hettie changed the subject. "Have you seen Will Stuart today?" Everyone was keeping well abreast of the changes up at Craigmore. The waste ground below Craigmore farm-steading was already being cleared. Two of Dod Moffat's tractors were in constant use, levelling the ground and carting away the spoil.

"He's a changed man," Dod Moffat said. "I hope the Bridge doesn't go out of business, for it'll be losing half its custom with him. Though they'll still get the other half from me."

"He was in here last night," Hettie said, "for half an hour, and he drank two sweet stouts." She sounded proud, almost as though it had been her own achievement to stop Will

276

Stuart's drinking. She smiled mistily. "I thought I'd never see that young laddie at the machine there again," she said, "but Will says he'll be back. He's back at home now. He's to take it easy, get plenty rest – common sense, that's all it is, you don't need doctors for that kind of thing. He wasn't bad hurt, bar a few cuts and bruises."

"He was hellish lucky," Dod Moffat said. "The mess Dave Simmers was in. Mind you, Sandy Thain thought his head was smashed in to begin with, with all the blood there was. But it seems it was just a cut in his scalp."

Hettie weighed up the emphasis Dod Moffat put on the word "seems". "A little blood goes a long way," she said.

"True enough, Hettie. But they're talking about the chance of other damage too."

"Damage?"

"He doesn't remember anything. The last he remembers is going up to Peter Ward's with me and his dad."

"It'll come back to him."

"I don't know. With some things it's maybe better if it doesn't come back."

Dod Moffat drained his glass.

Billy had begun to be bored and restive by the time he was allowed to go out and about. There was so little to do he would even have welcomed a shot at the fruit machine.

His father took him up to Craigmore. The waste of nettles below the steading was cleared away, scraped and levelled. A deep layer of hard-core was down, and smaller stones were being compacted in over the top now, a tractor and roller going backwards and forwards over them. The concrete foundations were down for a shed.

"Where's the old horse plough?" Billy asked.

His father shrugged. "On the Tip, I'd think. Why, did you want it?"

"There's an old horse plough outside a house at Culane. It's painted silver and green. It looks real fine."

A lorry edged in round the side of the steading. It backed onto the compacted stones. Slowly the back tipped up, higher, higher, the extending rod gleaming dully. The back flapped open, the grey blocks crunched down like dominoes shaken out of a box, the grey dust rising and subsiding round them. The lorry moved forwards, shaking the last blocks out onto the ground.

"Well," Will Stuart grinned, "I'd best get building."

For a moment, as he watched the lorry moving away, a sense came over Billy of the strangeness of the world. Drift was dead and Peter Ward was dead; and Dave Simmers was dead. The best and the worst. The old life was

passing – here, a new business starting, his
father was all energy and enthusiasm and
laughter. And what was this new business?
Scrap! The tail end of people's things, the
things they flung out, had no more use for, left
behind when they died or moved away. And
then they would be sorted through, to be made
into something new again. Billy screwed up his
eyes at the trees around the steading: they were
full of leaf, their new green was darkening,
filmed with grey dust.

A week after he had been discharged from hospital, Billy had a visit from Theresa Thain. He
saw her leaning her bike by the hedge and
wavering up the path to the front door. She
had a plastic bag under her arm. His first reac-
tion was to panic, to run and hide, to get away.
But an instant later he found himself going to
the door, and had opened it before she had
even reached it.

She said her mother had suggested coming
over to inquire after Billy's health, and she had
brought the records she'd promised. Billy
didn't remember anything about records, but
he recognized that it was required of him to sit
back and receive the first of his musical edu-
cation. He felt as if he were watching himself,
all the while, with a wry grin.

They talked indifferently, but with more
ease than Billy would have thought likely.

At one stage she looked up at him, with an almost surprised expression, and said, "Everyone says you weren't tied up. But you told us you were. Were you?"

Whenever she came out with something, suddenly, like that, her eyebrows shot up into high, arching curves and her eyes became impossibly round. Billy couldn't help feeling, when she did this, that she was mocking him. He was silent.

"You don't have to tell me if you don't want to," she said. There was a light smile on her lips. Something deep inside Billy whispered, Yes, you do want to.

"I'm not sure," he said at last, forcing a smile in return. "I seem to have forgotten a whole bit."

He had made a conscious decision to forget. He had made it while he was still in the hospital, after the first round of questioning. There had not been much to the questions at that stage, but Billy had sensed the urgency of those pudding-faced men in their grey or blue suits, had frozen at their pretence of friendliness. Distrust of the police was deeply ingrained in him. He sensed the trap, the steel prison; that he was a pawn in their game, a means for them to continue on their own particular quest for their own particular villain, to win their own little share of glory. He had played on the hospital sisters' protectiveness, opted out of the questioning, and done a lot of thinking. He had decided to forget.

The police knew something about Dave Simmers and Andy Gibbon and copper, that was obvious. Two weeks before, he would probably have helped them. Now everything was changed. Dave Simmers was dead. Andy Gibbon was the father of his friend. It had not been Geordie's fault that the friendship had ended. Even when he was rocked, as he often was, by his parents or the police with their sensible and obvious arguments about why he should try to search his memory, he would only have to concentrate on a dim, luminous country within him, where he lived with his own, inviolate, feelings; and his silence remained intact. His silence remained, even as all memory of that dim country faded.

Becoming friendly with Theresa Thain was to alter this. It was to happen gradually, over the weeks and months that followed.

"You should keep your girlfriend's records in better order," his mother said one day. "They'll get scratched like that."

That was the first he even noticed it. He stopped. Again there was that moment of panic: that word, "girlfriend". It seemed so final. The wall was crossed. But even afterwards Billy found he was looking at himself, quizzically, good-humouredly, acknowledging with a certain awkward shame and a cer-

281

tain fascination that she had wormed her way under his guard; that threads of feeling which had been cut loose on Drift's death were attaching themselves softly, inextricably, around her. She opened up glimpses in him, he saw her dwindling down the dark convoluted passages of his memory, he wanted to walk up the old hill-path from the Yard with her, and show her the Moss and Peter Ward's empty hut. It was as though they were related: Peter Ward was her grandfather. Above all, it was on her land that Drift was buried.

Two weeks after he was discharged from hospital, a knock came at the back door. Billy's mother opened it. It was Geordie Gibbon.

"Oh – Geordie." His mother looked surprised, a little embarrassed. "Well – come in," she said.

"I wondered if Billy was coming a walk," said Geordie as he came into the kitchen. He seemed subdued, but there was a kind of quiet confidence about him too.

Billy's mother seemed to know something about him that Billy didn't. "You can go if you want, Billy," she said.

"I – I don't know," he said. "OK, I'll go. Where?"

"Up the hill?

"OK."

"Just don't get up to anything," his mother said. "See that he doesn't, Geordie. He's supposed to be taking it easy."

Geordie grinned. A wan grin, as if it was an effort. They went out. They walked along the street in silence, through the village, through the gate, onto the old railway track.

It was a soft day without sun. There had been thunder the previous afternoon, breaking the fine spell. Now everything was grey and fresh, occasionally heavy showers of mild rain crossed, wilfully soaking one field and leaving its neighbour quite dry.

"Did you get stitches?" Geordie inquired.

"Twelve," said Billy. "They're out now."

"Were they itchy?"

"Aye. I kept getting a row from Mum for scratching them."

"She should have tied your hands."

Billy glanced quickly at Geordie. Was he trying to be funny? There was a wariness between them, like an electric fence, yet they were both trying to be natural.

"They're saying he tied me up," Billy said. "They're saying I told them that."

Geordie nodded, frowned. "I thought he was bringing you home."

Billy shrugged. "I suppose," he said.

"Treeza Thain said you'd told them you were being driven in the white van, not a car."

"I got a bit mixed up." The fence between

283

them was bristling. Ten thousand volts.

They walked on. They left the railway track, crossed three fields, and started up the narrow tarred road that was the first of Culane Hill. Billy had to stop occasionally. He was still not quite right. Geordie softened. "You've been through a lot," he said.

Billy looked at him curiously. It was such a strange thing to say, for Geordie. It was like a man speaking. There was something different about Geordie. What had he been through?

The grass was sodden, the track slippery with mud. Billy stopped, panting.

"We'll go back if you want," said Geordie.

"No, we'll go on up. I must be getting fat."

"Middle-age spread," Geordie said. "Your mum's cakes."

Higher they climbed. The green land spread wider behind them in the soft grey light. Here and there, turnip fields showed up, tight cords of green on chocolate brown, in squares among the lush land.

After a long silence, Billy said, "Nobody liked Dave Simmers."

"True. It must be a bit lonely."

They passed a group of sheep, lying in the grass, all faced the same way, all chewing, in unison.

"When I spoke to Treeza Thain," Geordie said suddenly, in a strangely husky voice, "that's what made me come to see you. She

284

said you needed me." He laughed, a little embarrassed.

Billy grunted.

"Have you heard about my dad?" Geordie went on.

"What about him?"

Geordie said nothing for a long while. They stopped. They gazed down over the bowl of the valley: their world, where people lived their lives, and farmers grew green things among the earth and stones, where things were stolen, and people died, and some people told the truth. They could make out the new Yard among the trees at Craigmore, a tiny splash of bright fawn among the green. The yellow fire of broom had long faded off the upper slopes of Craigmore Hill.

"They've pulled him in," Geordie said at last.

"When?"

"A week ago."

"Nobody told me! Was it about the—"

"We never knew anything about it. Dave Simmers was in on it – he might have got it going in the first place – but it was my dad really. He was caught with a load of copper pipes. Down in Nottingham. I suppose they got a tip-off from somewhere – maybe round here." There was no accusation in his voice, no bitterness: he was just stating facts. "It was a big thing, thousands of pounds. Mum was

285

telling me a bit about it last night."

Billy was tongue-tied.

"Mum said she doesn't think she'll be able to keep her job," Geordie added.

"Are they putting her out?"

"No. But how would you feel if your teacher was the wife of a crook?"

"Do you think your dad's a crook?" It was an amazing thought.

"I don't know. I'm really mixed up. I just think of him as my dad. But – he *is* a crook, isn't he? Even if he did do it all for us. Mum said he isn't a bad man, he just made a bad mistake. He thought he was helping us and he was really doing us harm."

"My dad's handled hot stuff as well, but I'd never—"

"That was just little things," Geordie cut in. "Petty. It wasn't like – organized. Mum says we'll probably have to go on Social Security now, we won't have much money. Maybe have to sell the house."

Billy looked down at his feet. He was speechless, waves of guilt crossing his mind. A thick mist of rain trailed over the land in front of them.

Suddenly Geordie seized the watch on his wrist. It was a spasmodic movement. He ripped at it, tearing the bracelet over his hand, leaving white scratches on his skin. Then he flung it, hard, down the steepest part of the hill. The dull silver thing glinted in the dull silver air. It disappeared in the wet grass.

"That was a good watch," Billy said calmly. "I'd have given my eye teeth for a watch like that."

"Go and get it then," Geordie said. "Anyone can have it that wants it."

But Billy turned and went on up the hill. He reached the Cairn, climbed slowly to the top. Geordie followed close behind.

Billy stood looking down at the gravel path that sloped into the burial chamber between its narrow banks. It was littered with sweet-papers and the pull-rings of old cans.

"Like the crack in your bum," Geordie murmured, coming alongside him. He stood a moment, then slipped his arm round Billy's shoulders. Billy reached his own arm round and grasped Geordie's shoulder. They stood like that a while, on the top of the Cairn, leaning together like a pair of old trees in the soft, quick air.